I0677847

BREAKING THE CYCLE

OF

A DYSFUNCTIONAL FAMILY

JASMINE MINTER

Published by:

WALKING MIRACLE PUBLISHING

WRITERJASMINEMINTER@GMAIL.COM

This is a work of fiction. All events and characters in this story are solely the product of the author's imagination. Any resemblance between any characters and situations presented in this book to any individuals, living or dead, or actual events, establishments, organizations or locale are purely coincidental.

Published by:

Jasmine Minter/ Walking Miracle Publishing: "Where life is given to blank pages"

WriterJasmineMinter@gmail.com

Twitter: JMINTER_5

Facebook: Writer Jasmine Minter

Edited by: Nikkea Smithers Email: rwabookclub@yahoo.com

Cover Design: James Pressley Email: Jamesdpressley@yahoo.com
Facebook: James Pressley

Printed in the USA by: Create Space Independent Publishing Platform

ISBN: 978-0692-41144-5

"The idea is to write so that people hear it and it slides through the brain and goes straight to the heart."

-Maya Angelou

Brianna, a recent college graduate returns to her hometown of Richmond, VA on a quest to break the cycle of her dysfunctional family's upbringing. Having no positive role model, Brianna struggles with thoughts of becoming just another statistic. Will she jeopardize it all to save her family or pursue her own joy and self worth...

Dedication:

To

My Best Friend

Nicole "Toosie" Jones

November 9, 1984- October 14, 1994

You are dearly missed

Acknowledgements

With special thanks:

To my Heavenly Father, for blessing me with the creativity to influence, encourage and make a difference. I thank you Lord for the experiences and lessons I've been given on this journey called life.

To all of my family and friends for your encouragement and support! I truly appreciate you all!

To my editor, Nikkea Smithers, for taking the time out of your busy schedule to review this project. Also James Pressley, for seeing my vision and creating a powerful cover.

To many of you who have sent emails, text messages, and social media post to me, sharing your support, thoughts and testimony.

To those who encouraged, provided and gave me a chance!

To you for taking the time to read this book, enjoy and be encouraged!

Jasmine Minter

A Message to My Readers

First I want to start by saying thank you for your support! I truly appreciate you for taking the time to read this amazing book! *Breaking the Cycle* was originally a screenplay I wrote two years ago. After writing my first fiction book "Pursuing Justice" I realized that God has blessed me with this incredible platform to make a difference. With that being said I decided to convert *Breaking the Cycle* into a book. *Breaking the Cycle of a Dysfunctional Family* is a powerful story that talks a lot about generational struggles that are being repeated in family cultures, such as physical abuse, drug addiction, incarceration and abandonment issues. I believe that *Breaking the Cycle* will speak to each individual (reader) in a different way. I want you to be able to feel and experience the challenges that each character had to endure. My main purpose for this book is that you find yourself and choose to walk your own path instead of following the footsteps of your generation.

CHAPTER ONE

HEAT from the sun pressed against my cap and gown, causing sweat to drip from my forehead. Graduation music sounded throughout the large stadium, filled with proud friends and family members. A day that is supposed to be celebrated left me miserable inside. Apparently the piece of paper that everyone is so overly excited about is supposed to make life easier. For who, I don't know. While the sun continued to melt my face I searched desperately for my family in the stands, only to be left disappointed. Tears began to collect at the corners of my eyes. I discreetly pushed them back with the palm of my hand, hoping no one would notice the pain in my eyes and humiliation on my face.

The guest speaker proudly announced my name, "Brianna Armstrong." I moved towards the podium, gripping both sides of my gown, thinking to myself, "I should have worn flats". All eyes were glued on me when I shook hands with the president and guest speaker, as I accepted my degree. Who knew that a girl from the rough streets of South, Richmond would one day graduate with a degree in film and with a 3.9 GPA? Well I made it, sad to say without the support of my mother or father. College didn't mean much to my family. Hell, getting married wasn't even a belief. The only cycle repeated in my family was drug addiction, physical abuse and serving time in jail.

At birth my father decided that I wasn't good enough to be called his daughter. I was told by my mother that he left the day after I was born. My mom raised me and my big sister, Jewel until I was about three then she left, leaving my grandmother to take care of us. Where I'm from being raised by your grandparents is the norm, which is probably the problem with society today. Children are being raised without their parents and sometimes it causes them to seek the wrong guidance.

I didn't see my mother as often as I should've typically, on holidays or special occasions so her absence wasn't a surprise to me. I was however, expecting my sister and grandmother to be there. They're my biggest supporters not including my nephew Ethan. I just hoped everything was okay back home. Growing up with my grandparents wasn't easy. Grandma Beatrice was the kind of woman that's little but very intimidating. She's very protective, funny, strict and quick to give a lecture about the goodness of the lord or curse you out! All depends on the situation I guess. Not to mention her favorite word was the N-word. Of course if she caught any of us using it we would be in trouble.

I must admit she's been my greatest teacher and biggest fan since I could remember. I don't know what I would do without her. Jewel is ten years older than me. She's the loud crazy sister. You know, easier to get along with until you mess with her family. Anything I needed she made sure it was taken care of. She sacrificed so much just so that I could go to college. I owed her big time! I couldn't forget about my nephew, Ethan. Words couldn't begin to describe what he meant to me. With those three behind me that's all the motivation I needed.

After graduation a huge crowd of people exchanged hugs and kisses in the parking lot. Pitiful ole me walked alone, carrying the only piece of paper that kept me away from my family for the past four years. Sometimes I wondered if it was worth it. Would I get that big time director's job or would I end up working a nine to five

barley making ends meet? One thing my grandfather always said,

"It's not about how much money you make but what you do with

your money."

He constantly reminded us to never get paid for what we did

but for what we knew. With or without that paper I planned to be

one of the greatest. I was not your average twenty-two year old. The

struggle was only motivation for me. I learned not to feel sorry for

myself because feeling sorry never changed anyone's situation. At

least no one I knew. I took life for what it was, a journey.

After working my way through a busy parking lot I finally

made it to my car. A little embarrassed by my backseat. I quickly

tossed my high heels in the back with the rest of my luggage and

shoes, adding on to the junk. An elderly woman from across the

parking lot yelled, "Brianna." It was Mrs. Cutler, one of my

professors. She waved until we made eye contact then strutted

towards me wearing a pencil shirt, nice silk blouse and a pair of

pointy toe pumps. Mrs. Cutler was one of the sweetest person I'd ever known, always positive and willing to help anyone in need. She was one of the few well educated black females I knew.

The year prior when my transmission blew out, Mrs. Cutler was kind enough to give me an old used car that was just sitting in her backyard. I thought it was crazy how a stranger would help you before your own family. All I could do is smile and take the moment in. She returned the smile then handed me a card and a dozen purple lilies, just before hugging me. "I am so proud of you Brianna. You did it!"

My smile grew wider, "Thanks Mrs. Cutler!"

Remembering I too had something for Mrs. Cutler, "Wait before I forget." I set the card and lilies on the passenger seat then reached for my purse that rested on the floor, taking out a card, "Here you go." She gave me a warm smile before taking the card. Just seeing how proud she was made me emotional. This lady had done more for me in four years than my mom had done in my entire twenty-two years. It had nothing to do with material things. The time she had invested in me meant so much more. My vision started to blur from the few tears that crowded the corner of my eyes as I reflected on my past. Mrs. Cutler was a little concerned so she asked what was wrong. My emotions must have grabbed a hold of my tongue because I was completely speechless. Standing there reminiscing on how far I'd come made me even more emotional.

Before wrapping her arms around me, Mrs. Cutler asked desperately again what was wrong with me. Shaking my head, I simple responded nothing. She wiped a few tears that rested on my cheek before repeating herself. That's when I confessed that I wished that my grandmother could have been in attendance. I told her that my grandmother didn't drive and then lied about my mother having to work. It was no way I could tell Mrs. Cutler, I hadn't spoken to my mom since freshman year or that my father abandoned me at birth, so I lied.

Mrs. Cutler respond like she always did, positively by saying my grandmother and parents were very proud of me. "Yea right," I thought to myself. She continued by saying if she had a daughter like me she would be proud. She went on by saying I was beautiful, intelligent and very ambitious and not to let anyone tell me different.

"You deserve this Brianna, be proud" she said.

I smiled as my tears dissolved, "Thanks Mrs. Cutler." She smiled and gave me one last hug before parting away.

Once in the car I noticed a missed call and voice message from Grandma Beatrice. Excited, I immediately checked my voice mail to hear her sweet voice, "Hey Baby, its Grandma! I just wanted to tell you how sorry I am for missing your big day. My baby graduated from college (in her country accent), Lord- Jesus! I sho' am proud of you baby! Yes indeed! Well if you plan on driving back tonight, make sure you fill up your tank before hitting that highway and stay off that damn cellular phone while you driving. Alright baby, talk to you later."

I lowered the phone from my ear, placing it on speaker. I just knew I had to call her back. The phone rang three times before she answered.

"Hello."

"Hey Grandma."

Barely hearing me she repeats herself, "*Hello*."

"Hey Grandma. It's Brianna."

"Oh hey baby, I didn't know who you was, you here?"

Laughing at her response, "No Grandma, I'm about to leave South Carolina now and head to Richmond."

Hysterical she asks, "Oh Lord, you driving?"

"Yes," I answered.

"Well why the hell you on the phone then?" she yelled through the phone. I held the phone in silence, afraid to answer. Her worried voice grows louder, "I told you about being on that phone while you're driving. You're hard headed. You know police giving out tickets now in Virginia to people that text and drive."

"Grandma, I'm not texting." I replied.

She takes a deep breath, "It's doesn't matter! You're not supposed to be on that phone while you're driving either, it's dangerous."

I attempted to speak, "But… Grandma…"

Her voice over powered mine, "I'm getting off this phone. I'll see you when you get here."

"Hold on Grandma, I'm pulling up at the gas station now."

Rudely she says, "And!" She goes on by telling me the risk of pumping gas while talking on the phone. She'd always been so superstitious. "You could blow something up!" She yelled through the phone. Giggling at her response the call suddenly got disconnected. I couldn't stop laughing at the fact that she hung up in my face.

The next morning after a long night of driving I was awakened by the aroma of cooked bacon. Slowly I pulled back the covers and stepped out of my iron brass antique twin size bed that my grandmother had since my mother was a kid. The floor squeaked as I tip toed around bags of luggage and shoe boxes to reach the bedroom door. I freshened up a bit before heading downstairs to the kitchen.

When I entered the kitchen I saw my grandma by the stove, with her favorite wig on, covering up her beautiful gray hair, wearing her worn down pink bathrobe with the rugged strings hanging from the bottom. While humming one of her favorite Gospel songs as she cooked breakfast. "Morning Grandma," I said greeting her as I entered the kitchen.

She turned to notice me, dropping the fork on the counter, rushing over to hug and kiss me, "Hey baby, come here." She hugged me tighter and pinched my cheeks

"Ouch, Grandma, dang", I yelled in slight pain.

 "Oh hush Brianna!" She looked me up and down proud, "Look at my graduate." She says smiling. "What time you get in last night" she asked.

"A little past mid-night."

Her bottom lip dropped to the floor, "Lord Jesus and you up this early?" Tickled by her response I told her I couldn't resist the smell of the swine. That's when she encouraged me to relax in the family room until breakfast was ready.

17

Seeing all the pictures alongside of the hallway of me and my sister brought back so many memories from childhood. Once I reached the family room I could tell nothing had changed. Her antique sofa was still covered in plastic, family portraits flooded the walls and plants were everywhere. Glancing over the room I discovered my grandparent's wedding picture.

My grandfather passed away six years prior, from a stroke, just two years before I left for college. He was so funny and laid back. Sometimes his sense of humor would get him in trouble with my grandmother. I really missed having him around. They had been married for 49 years before he passed away. It was hard leaving Grandma Beatrice in that big house by herself while I went away to school but Jewels refused to let me turn down a full scholarship. Instead she promised to take care of Grandma Beatrice while I was away.

Later that afternoon, I went to AJ's auto shop to get an oil change. While in the waiting area I noticed this guy staring at me from across the room. We made eye contact each time I glanced up from my phone. He looked mean from his facial expressions but sort of cute at the same time. You know the type that never smiles but was still attractive. Twenty minutes had passed and my car was finally ready. After paying I was headed out the door until a voice yelled from behind, "Excuse me." I stopped in my footsteps and turned to notice the same guy that was staring at me. He approached me wearing a wife beater with a towel hanging from his shoulder. I assumed he was a mechanic from the oil stains on his pants.

He smiled for the first time saying, "Hey, how you doing?" I gave him a weird look as if I wasn't interested. I said hi, gave him a fake smile then continued to my car. "Hold on for a second Ms?" I acted as if I didn't hear him but he was persistent, as he followed me to my car. "I was wondering if I could call you sometime." He asked.

I turned to him and replied, "Do you ask every female who comes into the shop for their number?"

"Only the rude ones," he said laughing as I gave him an unpleasant stare. "I'm just joking. I'm Chase by the way. Listen, I'm not trying to run game on you. I just think you're beautiful and if

19

given the time I would like to take you out for coffee." Immediately I told him I didn't drink coffee.

In the middle of our conversation a really nice car pulled up and parked beside me with a license plate that read AJ Auto. I anticipated that it was the owner of the shop. A man steps out of the car wearing a really nice sweat suit carrying a gym bag. He spoke and continued into the shop. Right before I got into my car Chase reached into his back pocket, pulled out his wallet and handed me his business card, "I hope to hear from you" he said smiling. I took the card, got into the car and drove off.

After leaving the shop I made my way to Jewels' house to visit her and Ethan. When I pulled up to her building I noticed a group of men crowding the hallway. The sun was blazing so most of the guys were shirtless. When I walked towards Jewel's apartment I was approached by Markell, a guy I knew from my childhood. "What's up girl," he said in his country Virginia accent.

Surprised I replied, "Oh my God, Markell! How are you?" We both hugged each other. "I'm good, just working." He said with a smile.

"Okay, well it's good to see you." Just when I moved closer to Jewel's front door, Markell asked how Grandma Beatrice was doing.

He mentioned that he knew she hadn't been feeling well lately. My face had confused written all over it. I told him she was doing okay. He replied cool, not knowing I was completely unaware of Grandma Beatrice illness. I knocked a few times before entering Jewel's apartment.

As soon as I turned the knob I saw Ethan in an oversized t-shirt, sitting in the floor, watching cartoons. My heart smiled. "Ethan," I called. He turned to me then leapt up then gave me a huge hug. I glanced over the room, wondering where Jewel was. I found a seat on the couch. Ethan followed and climbed onto my lap. "Where's your mom?" I asked.

His sweet little voice replied, "In there" pointing to the back room.

Jewel entered the living room, wearing a bathrobe and bonnet on her head. She patted her head a couple times to decrease the itch. "Hey Bri girl, when you get here?" She says as she continues to pat her head.

I began tickling Ethan, "Not too long ago." I replied. Then a shirtless man, with gold teeth that looked to be in his late 20's, approached Jewel from behind and hugged her inappropriately. This guy was in serious need of a shave and belt. Jewel laughed at his behavior. I quickly turned Ethan's head in the opposite direction. The guy then moved to the kitchen, grabbed a beer from the refrigerator then returned to the back room.

Jewel sat down on the couch across from us. She lit a cigarette then turned to me and said, "What you got planned for today?" She took a puff then crossed her legs, while waiting for my response.

I told her I wanted to spend some time with Ethan so I planned to take him to Belles Island for a few hours to chill by the river. Jewel seemed to be relieved, stating that she could use the break. She took another puff from the cigarette before asking had I spoken to my mom. The smoke made her cough. I waved my hand to keep the smoke from reaching Ethan's face.

"No I haven't spoken to Debbie," I said as I lifted Ethan from my lap. "Go put some clothes on baby so we can go by the river." He said okay and ran eagerly to his room.

Once Ethan left I confronted Jewel, "So who is this guy and when did you start smoking? And why are you smoking around Ethan?"

Jewel put the cigarette out in the ashtray that rested on the coffee table in front of us. "What's with all the questions?" Jewel replied.

I nodded my head, "Okay, how long have you two been dating?"

Giggling she replied, "I'm not dating him. He's just a friend."

I rolled my eyes and crossed my legs, "You let all your friends sleep over?" I asked.

She gave me the evil eye and said, "That's none of your business." I shook my head disappointed. "Brianna, lighten up, gosh!" She yelled.

"You shouldn't have men in and out of your house especially with Ethan here." I said as I stood to my feet.

"Okay, Brianna!" She replied boldly, cutting me off. "Dee is my boyfriend. I've been seeing him for a few months now."

Just as I was about to tell Jewel off, Ethan returned fully dressed. "I'm ready" He said. As Ethan reached for my hand we both exited the apartment and carefully walked down the flight of stairs. I was disappointed in Jewel. That wasn't like her to have anybody around Ethan. Jewel was a strong woman but she had always been weak when it came to men. It's like she had to feel wanted or something.

When we reached the bottom of the stairs the number of guys had expanded. I walked timidly through the crowd while Ethan

24

followed, holding my hand. Markell gave me a head nod as we passed through. All I could think about was Grandma Beatrice's health.

CHAPTER TWO

Later that night after unpacking my clothes, everything was well organized in my closet. As I prepared for bed the phone rung. I walked over to the night stand where the phone rested and *"Debbie"* displayed on the screen. I really didn't want to be bothered with my mom so I stared at the phone, contemplating if I should answer or not. I hadn't spoken to her since we got into a huge argument after my Grandpa's funeral because she came there drunk. She tried calling me several times while away at school but I just couldn't get pass everything she'd done to me and my sister.

The phone rung again right before I decided to pick up, "Hello."

Excited she replied, "Hey Brianna."

I laid across the bed and took a deep breath before responding, "Hey." She went on to say how proud she was of me for graduating from college. I moved the phone from my ear and stared at it with a disgusted look on my face and said thanks. I really didn't have much to say so I kept my words short and sweet. I guess she could tell because she made up some story about me sounding tired so she would call me later. I said okay and quickly hit the end button faster then she could say good-bye. I was still hurting from things she'd done in the past. Tears streamed down my face faster than an avalanche. I tossed the phone onto the nightstand then cried myself to sleep while in the fetal position.

The next morning, I woke up determined to know the truth about Grandma Beatrice's health. After bathing I headed to the kitchen where I found her sitting at the table, sipping from her favorite mug while watching the local news. "Hey Grandma", I said as I entered the kitchen.

She glanced up and greeted me with a smile as I leaned over to place a kiss on her cheek. She then asked if I wanted anything to eat. I said yes and moved towards the stove but she insisted on making my plate for me. She placed her mug on the table, moved me out the way then went on to preparing my food while I sat down at the table.

When she handed me my plate I didn't waste any time. I started reaching for food before she could put the plate on the table. Disturbed, Grandma Beatrice yelled, "Brianna, you know better!"

I was confused so I said, "What?" Before I knew it she raised her arm pretending to hit me. Completely unsure if she was serious or not, I flinched back but she caught herself. I couldn't help but to laugh, "What Grandma?" I asked again, not knowing what she was upset about.

Her eyes grew wider as she stood over me, resting her hands on her hip, "You answer me what again, you gonna be picking your teeth off the floor."

I told her I was sorry for being disrespectful. I was just hungry, but I guess my explanation wasn't good enough because she continued to preach saying, "You know better than to eat your food without blessing it. I raised you better than that Brianna." Ashamed, I slowly bowed my head, trying to disguise the smirk on my face so I could pray. I noticed Grandma Beatrice wasn't eating so I asked if she was hungry but she said no. It was a little strange to me because she hadn't eaten a full meal since I returned home. I started to wonder if her illness had anything to do with her appetite.

While eating breakfast the local news displayed a murder investigation that happened the night before. "Lord Jesus," Grandma Beatrice shouted, "This is the fourth killing this week and it's only Tuesday."

I shook my head while saying, "Richmond is getting terrible Grandma."

She disagreed, "No it's just a bunch of lost souls out here, that's what it is. A lot of these young folks don't have positive role models to look up to." Determined, she continued to get her point across, "Now, I'm not making excuses for these young folks and their foolish behaviors but it's a lot of fatherless children out here looking for guidance from the wrong people. You have these young girls turning to the wrong men for love and these young boys turning to the streets.

Let me tell you something baby, you're gonna meet a lot of men that desire you but only a few will value you! Remember that! A real man appreciates quality, yes indeed." She took a sip from her mug and continued, "Bets believe we're living in the last days, ancestors probably turning over in their graves the way these young folks carrying on. I remember when black folks couldn't even try on a pair of shoes in the store and now these young folks killing each other over tennis shoes and going to jail over non-sense. In my day people got arrested for things they believed in, like the right to vote. Now young folks are just going to jail and losing their right to vote. We have to do better as a society. History is repeating itself, don't you see? Cops killing people, bodies being found hung from trees. You young folks need to wake up because the future is depending on you!"

I could always count on Grandma Beatrice to give me some knowledge on history. She was the one who told me that Richmond had one of the largest slave holding facilities. Grandma Beatrice also told me that black history didn't start with slavery, that's what the school system taught us. She would say, "As human beings we believe what we are taught so always get the facts first Brianna. Higher learning is very important but self-education is just as important." One of my favorite stories she told was about a man who mailed himself in a wooden box from Virginia to Philadelphia to be free from slavery. I loved that story. It takes a lot of courage to do something like that. Hell it seemed like I learned more about history from Grandma Beatrice than I did from the public school system. That's what I loved about her she was always educating us.

While finishing up my breakfast the news then exposed a picture of a young lady that looked very familiar. I couldn't recall her name but I knew I went to high school with her. Turns out her mom found her dead outside of their home. I heard she overdosed on prescription pills. Confused Grandma Beatrice asks, "Prescription drugs?" I explained to her that people were taking pills to get high now days. Grandma Beatrice then gave me this surprising look, "What?" she says. "When did this start, I don't even like taking medicine when I'm sick and you think I'm going to take a pill to catch a buzz." I laughed.

"Lord Jesus and I thought reefer was bad" she said as I giggled and told her I never heard of anyone dying from smoking weed. She gave me a grin, "You said that like you smoke reefer."

Humored by her comment I replied, "No ma'am not me. I'm just stating the facts."

She then stared me up and down and said, "You better not be." She went on speaking about the risk of taking drugs and how young folks better be careful because popping pills could lead to other things. She then stated, "Once your body becomes immune to one drug it stops having the same effect and that's usually when folks start seeking stronger things, like heroin or crack."

Chuckling I replied, "Crack, really Grandma?"

She shrugs, "Okay, I guess I was born yesterday and I don't know anything."

I smiled, "I didn't say that Grandma, but speaking of health, what's going on with you?"

She pretended like she didn't have a clue what I was talking about. "What do you mean?" she asked. That's when I told her I knew about her illness. She replied nonchalant, "I am fine baby." Then she walked over to the sink to start the dish water.

After washing dishes she returned to the table placing her hand over mines. She looked at me, took a deep breath and told me something that I wasn't prepared to hear, "Baby, I have Cirrhosis of the liver."

I didn't really understand what that meant so I asked to be sure. Cirrhosis of the liver was basically when the liver stopped working properly. "You use to drink grandma?" I asked, hoping it wasn't true.

Before answering, she turns away then said, "Yes." At this point I was unable to think clear. I took a deep breath, rested my elbow on the table and covered my face with my hand. Grandma Beatrice comforted me by rubbing my leg. I never seen my grandmother pick up a bottle, let alone drink from one. She removed my hands from my face and began to explain, "Before I took full responsibility of you and Jewel, I use to be an alcoholic. I would drink two-three, maybe four glasses of liquor a day, if not more. At the time I was dealing with some infidelity issues with your grandfather." She paused for a second before continuing, "Brianna, you girls saved my life and my marriage. If your mom had not left you and your sister with me I probably wouldn't be alive today.

"The day Debbie dropped you girls off I knew I had to make some changes in my life and putting the bottle down was one. I wanted the best for my grand-babies so from that day forward I started attending AA meetings for help. Your grandfather made some changes too. Yes he did. He stopped messing around and started being the husband that I needed. Things got better for the both of us when you two moved in. That's when I realized that my situation wasn't about me but the plan God had for my life. Sometimes added responsibility can be beneficial to your situation. You just never know what the Lord has in store for you, sugar. What may seem like a disaster to you may be a blessing for someone else."

I interrupted her before she could say another word, "No, you guys saved me and Jewel." I yelled holding back tears. "Who knows where we would've been if you and Grandpa hadn't taken us in. I still can't believe Debbie just left us like that."

Grandma Beatrice hated when I called my mom by her first name but I just didn't feel comfortable calling her mom. "Wait a minute now" She said. "Before you go talking bad about your mommy, you need to know why she did what she did." I really wasn't trying to hear anything Grandma Beatrice had to say about Debbie. I smacked my lips when she tried to explain my mother's reason for leaving us. It was a bit disrespectful of me but I was only expressing my true feelings. Grandma Beatrice continued by telling me to watch my mouth and that I should always show respect towards my mother because she birthed me.

"Brianna your mother did what she felt was best for you and Jewel at the time" she said as she reached for my hand. "You need to talk to her to get the full truth before judging her. Hell, I don't blame her for what she did."

Irritated I turned to her and said, "How can you say that Grandma, she abandoned us?"

Grandma Beatrice was offended by my response. I attempted to speak but her voice over powered mine, "You're so stubborn,

Brianna. If you never listen you'll never hear anything. You need to call her and find out the truth."

"For what Grandma!" I yelled. "I don't want anything to do with her."

"Don't say that Brianna" she replied.

"Grandma I can't help how I feel."

She took a deep breath and said, "Honey, you need to learn how to forgive because you're not hurting anybody but yourself. Life is a journey with many lessons. You're supposed to make mistakes. Give your mommy a chance and stop carrying the pain of your past in your heart and forgive her."

"Forgive her! Why should I do that?" I asked. "That's not going to change what she's done."

Grandma Beatrice shook her head and said it a low tone, "No, it won't change the past but it will heal that bitter heart of yours." I took a deep breath and continued to listen to Grandma Beatrice go on and on about my no good mother. She said, "Sugar, you have to learn not to expect everyone in your life to be perfect because let me tell you something child, no one is. Do yourself a favor and forgive yourself. Learn how to do what's right on purpose. If you do what you're supposed to do your feelings will follow along. Let God deal with your enemies! If you keep trying to take care of everything God can't take care of you."

My emotions were all over the place. I wanted so badly to cry but my pride wouldn't let me. Then Grandma Beatrice leaned over to me and said, "Baby, I know it's hard but you have to forgive people that hurt you. Usually when people hurt you it's because they're hurting. You just never know what a person is going through. Honey, the best thing you can do when somebody hurt you is pray for them. What if everybody judged you on your past, how would you feel? Don't forget what Jewel did for you. Remember no one is perfect."

I looked my Grandma directly in the eyes and said, "The things that happened in my past weren't my fault."

She looked at me and said, "I'm not saying that they were but it still happened and no one is judging you."

Jasmine Minter

CHAPTER THREE

The next day Grandma Beatrice had a doctor's appointment. I was a little concerned about her health, especially with her lack of eating and ankles swelling so I tagged along. While waiting for the doctor I browsed-through a couple magazines at the same time Grandma Beatrice worked on a crossword puzzle.

"Good Morning," the doctor said as he entered the room greeting us both with a smile.

He placed his chart onto the counter then turned to me, "And who is this young lady" He asked.

I stood to my feet and extended my arm to shake his hand, "Hi, I'm Brianna, her granddaughter."

He reached for my hand, "Well hello Miss. Brianna, it's nice to meet you!"

I returned the smile, "You too" I replied.

He turned to Grandma Beatrice, "And how are you doing today Mrs. Adams?"

Grandma sat the crossword puzzle to the side and said, "I'm making it."

The doctor then reached for his chart and glanced over it, "So how are you feeling Mrs. Adams?" Grandma Beatrice responded confidently like everything was okay. I knew how much my Grandma hated the doctor so even if she was hurting she wouldn't say it. She told him she felt great but I knew that was a lie. Before the doctor could ask any more questions I told him about her lack of eating, her ankles swelling and her being short of breath lately.

Grandma Beatrice was upset by my response. She gave me this *I can't believe you just said that* kind of look before firmly responding, "Hush Brianna, there's nothing wrong with me. I am just fine." She then mumbled under her breath, "Shut the hell up." before turning to the doctor, "Excuse my granddaughter, she's a little over protective. There's nothing wrong with me. I just eat smaller potions now and my ankles usually swell when I stand on my feet too long."

The doctor asked more questions, "Have you been following your diet?" At this point Grandma Beatrice seemed very disturbed. I kept quiet so she wouldn't fuss at me. That's when the doctor reminded her of the importance of following her diet right before checking her vital signs.

On the ride home I asked Grandma Beatrice what was her secret to staying so strong and calm during sickness. She simply replied, "Honey, I may struggle but I'll never quit! My secret to staying calm during difficult situation is simple, I pray." My Grandma was so strong I hoped to have her strength one day.

During the drive I received a call from Debbie but of course I couldn't answer even if I wanted to because Grandma Beatrice didn't like when I talked on the phone while I was driving. I didn't have much to say to her anyway so I ignored the call.

Thirty seconds later the phone rang again. I glanced down at the screen and it was Debbie calling once again. Grandma Beatrice then asked who kept calling. When I told her it was my mom she insisted that I answer. I was surprised at her response being that I was driving. "Grandma I thought you didn't like when I talk on the phone and drive?"

She thought for a second, "Well cut it off! I'm tired of hearing it ring! Call her back when you get to the house."

My face frowned up, "I don't want to talk to her." I replied. Once I said that Grandma drilled me about respecting my elders and always respecting my parents no matter what. I tried explaining that I had nothing to say to Debbie but Grandma Beatrice didn't care, she continued to speak her mind.

My mom took me and Jewel through a lot and I didn't think I was ready to have a conversation with her. Have you ever hated a person so much that you couldn't stand to be in the same room as them? Well that's how I felt about Debbie. She should have been there for us instead of running the streets getting high and drunk. Grandma Beatrice begged me to call her later so I said ok to hush her up but before I knew it the phone rang again so I answered, "Hello."

I guess she was little surprised that I picked up because she was speechless for a second, "Hello, Bri."

I replied careless, "Hey." She then asked how I was doing. I told her I was fine then breathed hard through the phone to indicate that I was annoyed. She then asked bravely if we could meet to talk. I admit, I was disgusted with the choices Debbie made in the past but I was still curious to know why. During the conversation she was acting as if we had a great mother-daughter relationship so I told her what was on my mind, "You just left us," I yelled through the phone. "What kind of mother leaves her children?"

She was offended by my words so she tried to flip the script on me, "What makes my situation any different from yours Brianna? Jewel told me everything!" I was so over her so I hung up the phone and turned the volume up on the radio.

Later that night, Jewel decided to stay over. Ethan fell asleep on the couch so we both slept with Grandma Beatrice for old times' sake. The entire night we laughed and joked about Grandma Beatrice's worn out wig that needed to be tossed in the garbage.

While we giggled amongst each other Grandma Beatrice demanded us to go to sleep. Jewel laughed so hard that she could barely speak. Still giggling she asked Grandma Beatrice when she was going to get a new wig so she could toss the old one. I couldn't hold my laugh in so I busted out laughing and said, "Yesss, because that one is done!"

Grandma Beatrice got a little offended so she turned to Jewel and said, "You're not throwing anything away."

I yelled from the other side of the bed, "I'll do it for you."

That's when she yelled, "You touch my wig and I'm going to break your fingers. We couldn't stop laughing. When Grandma Beatrice turned her back to us I decided to bravely get out of bed without making a sound and hide her wig in Jewel's bag. This was the most fun we had in years together. Usually the only time we get together is for funerals.

The next morning Grandma Beatrice woke up before the both of us. I could smell breakfast cooking from the bedroom. Jewel was sound asleep so I left her alone and made my way into the kitchen. I noticed Grandma Beatrice wearing one of her newer wigs. I guessed she couldn't find the one I hid in Jewel's bag.

"Hey Grandma," I said as I entered the kitchen.

She cut her eyes at me and says, "Don't hey me! Where is my wig Brianna?"

I tried so hard to keep a serious face. "Your wig?" I asked as if I had no idea.

"Yes, my wig" she yelled.

I couldn't tell her that I took her wig because if I did who knows what she'd do me. I tried complimenting her new wig, hoping she would forget the old one but she continued to ignore me. I thought it was funny so I started to laugh. Grandma Beatrice on the other hand was dead serious about finding her wig. Sternly she said, "My wig better be back on my manikin tomorrow morning or I'm beating you and your sister's ham-pots." I was amused by her response but I was too afraid to laugh. Instead I told her I was grown and she couldn't touch me.

Before I knew it she rushed towards me. I quickly jumped from my chair and ran to the other side of the kitchen table, laughing nonstop. She couldn't catch me so she gave up, "Go wake Ethan up and tell him to sit on that commode before he has an accident on my couch." She demanded. "And get them tennis shoes out of my kitchen."

I laughed, "Grandma its 2014, their called sneakers not tennis and it's called a toilet not a commode." She waved me off as she continued into the family room to fold clothes.

Jewel finally woke up and entered the kitchen. Mean mug on her face and bonnet on her head wearing a huge t-shirt she had borrowed from Grandma Beatrice the night before.

"Where's Grandma?" She asked while yawning and stretching her arms.

I continued eating while pointing in the direction of the family room. I whispered as she walked towards the table, "She knows that we have her wig."

Jewel starts laughing then asks, "What'd she say?" I explained to Jewel the consequences if we didn't return the wig but she just waved me off and said, "Whatever."

During breakfast Jewel asked me why I hung up in Debbie's face the day before. I stopped eating and glanced up and asked who told her. She laughed and said, "Mom told me everything." My entire mood changed when Jewel started talking about Debbie. Jewel just kept going on and on about how I needed to reach out to her but all I could think about was her leaving us. Jewel then tried to convince me by saying, "No one is perfect, not even you Bri. You were too young to understand anything that happened between Mom and Dad back in the days."

The moment she said Dad I gave Jewel this awkward look. All my life I was told my dad left the day after I was born but, I guess I had the story wrong. Jewel told me that my mother's drug addiction didn't start until she started having problems with our father.

Sarcastically I asked, "Mom was a crack head?"

Jewel didn't find me too funny. She gave me and evil look and said, "Bri I'm serious! You need to call mom. Just like you had some tough decisions to make before leaving for college, mom had to do the same. I forgave her, why can't you?"

I was offended that Jewel would even compare my situation to Debbie's. I was nothing like her. No one could ever say anything that would change the way I felt about Debbie. Jewel tried her best to make me feel bad so I told her what was on mind, "Mom did what she did, now she has to live with it. Don't try to come at me about my situation. Do I ever say anything about you and Dee?"

Jewel hated that I mentioned her *boyfriend*. She went on saying that Dee had nothing to do with the situation. I rolled my eyes and said, "You want to talk about me and my imperfect life so let's talk about you and your no good boyfriend. By the way is he still asking you for money and not giving you anything in return but sex? What kind of man sits around all day and does nothing while his lady is out working."

"Bri, you're going too far now." She continued by saying, "I know my life is not perfect and I never said it was but don't try to hurt me because you're hurting! Don't forget if it wasn't for me you wouldn't have a college degree! I put my life on hold for you and this is how you repay me? You need to get your emotions in control, call mom and tell her how you feel! Stop trying to make other people feel bad because you're miserable!"

At this point I was done talking to Jewel so I got up from the table and attempted to leave but Jewel reached for my hand and said, "Bri all I'm asking is for you to give mom a chance. People change you know. Give her a call and hear what she has to say." I waited for Jewel to finish then walked away.

Jasmine Minter

CHAPTER FOUR

Later that day I took Ethan to the park while Jewel worked. As I pushed Ethan on the swings I heard a voice from behind say, "Well hello."

When I turned around I noticed Chase, the guy form the car shop. "So you're stalking me now" I asked.

He giggled, "Maybe." I walked over to the nearest bench and sat down while Ethan continued to swing. Chase joined me, "What are the odds that I run into you at the park?" He asked.

I watched Ethan from the bench as I replied, "Pretty high if you're following me."

He smiled and asked, "So why haven't I heard from you?"

I turned to him and laughed, "Who said I was gonna call?"

Sounds of the Ice cream truck played throughout the park. Ethan jumped from the swing and ran over, asking for money to get ice cream. I grabbed a dollar from my pocket and gave it to him. As

Ethan ran towards the truck I followed just steps behind. Chase walked over to me and said, "Cute kid, that's your son?"

I stared at Ethan before responding, "No, he's my nephew."

Shocked Chase replied, "Really! Wow, ya'll got some strong genes."

I quickly changed the subject, "Enough about my nephew, what brings you to the park?"

Before Chase answered I could feel him staring. He smiled. "I come here to play ball so I can stay in shape." I looked him up and down. He was very fit and seemed to be well in shape.

In the middle of our conversation my phone rang. I glanced down to notice Debbie's name on the screen. I didn't want to be bothered by her so I pressed ignored then there was a call from Jewel right after, "Hello?" I answered.

Jewel's voice sound as if she was in distress, "You need to get to the hospital" she said.

Barely hearing her, I repeated "Hospital?" That's when she told me that Grandma Beatrice had to be rushed to the emergency room. I hung up the phone, "Look I have to go." I said as I pulled Ethan from the line.

Concerned, Chase asked, "Everything okay with you, lady?"

I shook my head, "No, my Grandmother is in the hospital. Come on Ethan, we have to go!" As we rushed to the car Chase stood there unsure of what to do.

When I arrived at the hospital I found most of my family in the waiting room crying and hugging. Jewel's head lifted from Dee's chest when she saw me. As I moved closer to her I could see Jewel's face drenched in tears. She looked at me speechless, shaking her head from left to right. I knew then that Grandma Beatrice was gone. I wrapped my arms around Ethan. I just stood there in disbelief. I could feel my heart shatter into a thousand pieces. Jewel rubbed my back hoping to soothe the pain. Then she said, "Brianna, its ok to cry." But I was too angry to cry. I couldn't believe it, we were just joking the night before and she seemed fine. I don't get it. Grandma always talked about trusting God but all He seemed to ever do was take away the people I loved the most. How could I trust someone who always disappoints me?

"What happen?" I asked Jewel. She inhaled then exhaled slowly stating that Debbie called 911 when she saw that Grandma Beatrice was vomiting and having chest pain. I was confused because the doctor didn't mention that Grandma Beatrice was on her death bed during her last visit. The doctor approached us explaining that the liver was severely damaged. When I asked him why Grandma Beatrice wasn't aware of her illness he told us that she knew about her condition a year ago. According to the doctor Grandma Beatrice asked that he didn't disclosed any information to friends or family regarding her health. Jewel and I both looked at each other, devastated. The doctor cleared his throat and gave us his deepest condolences.

The next morning when I woke up, Jewel was in the kitchen talking on the phone. When she got off she asked me if I was okay. I said yes, but truth be told I really wasn't. My grandmother was the only person I could talk to about anything. I needed her and she was gone. It seemed like everyone I loved always ended up leaving me. It felt like I was cursed or something. It just was not fair. I couldn't understand why Jewel hadn't told me about Grandma Beatrice's illness sooner. I joined her at the table seeking an explanation. She went on about Grandma Beatrice begging her not to tell me. I rolled my eyes and said, "Whatever."

Jewel apologized several times but it didn't matter to me because Grandma Beatrice was already gone. She went on to say that it was the perfect time to call our mom. I told her I didn't want anything to do with our no good mother. Jewel didn't like when I talked bad about Debbie. She told me to watch my mouth. I explained that I was only telling the truth. Jewel then looked at me and said, "Bri you have to stop holding things in, you're not hurting anyone but yourself. I know how hard it could be to forgive a person who hurt you. It took me years to forgive our father but I did.

"When Mom was pregnant with you, her and Dad's relationship was pretty rocky. She wasn't working at the time so she really depended on him financially. Instead of coming home on payday he left us in the house every other weekend with not much to

57

eat. I remember on one particular Friday Mom decided to take a little visit where Dad hung out at, which was a gambling spot not too far from where we lived. When we got there, Dad was walking out the door drinking a beer. Mom immediately parked the car, grabbed me and marched towards him. They argued for about fifteen minutes then Dad started to walk away. I was so young and naïve. I thought he could do no wrong so I followed behind, hoping he would take me with him. Instead he kept telling me to go back with Mom then before I knew it he pushed me. It wasn't a hard push but it was hard enough to make me cry. That night was the last time I begged for his love. It wasn't until later years that I forgave him so believe me when I say; I understand how hard it is to forgive a person. You forgiving Mom won't make what she's done right or justify it but it will free you from resentment."

CHAPTER FIVE

A month went by and we were still mourning the loss of Grandma Beatrice. The house just wasn't the same anymore. While packing her things I noticed a journal tucked away in her dresser draw under a pile of clothes. It was the journal I kept in high school. Browsing through it brought back so many memories, both good and bad. Finding the journal reminded me why I wanted to become a filmmaker. I wanted to be able to tell stories like no one else could. I wanted people to not only relate or be entertained by my stories but grow and change the way they think. That journal was a sign to stay focused on my agenda. I could still hear the sound of Grandma Beatrice's voice as if she was still there saying, "The moment you know who you are is the moment you'll know what you could do. Use your pain and struggles as motivation to find your passion and purpose." Those words really stuck with me. Losing Grandma Beatrice was hard but it gave me the strength to pursue my dreams.

While cleaning there was a knock at the front door. When I went to open it, there she was, the woman who abandoned me. Debbie was an alcoholic and a recovering drug addict. She walked around feeling guilty for herself. I personally thought she was a worthless woman who wanted people to feel sorry for her too, but I wouldn't do it.

We stood silent in the doorway before she decided to speak. I looked at her and returned to packing, leaving her standing there. She closed the door and followed behind. She stood there for a second glancing around the room then finally asked, "You almost finish packing?"

I continued to pack and waited a few seconds before responding, "I wish. I didn't realize Grandma had so much stuff." I said.

She found a seat on the couch asking if we could talk. I moved a few boxes and told her I thought that's what we were doing. She shook her head and stared at the floor, "Brianna you know what I'm talking about." She said.

"Honestly, I don't think there's anything to discuss" I replied.

Debbie smiled sarcastically, "Honey you have no idea what you're talking about and that's why we need to talk."

I tried having a conversation with her without arguing but she kept pressing all of the wrong buttons. I dropped everything, and turned to her and yelled, "Okay you want to talk, let's talk. Why did you leave us?"

She looked at me with a hurtful stare. Tears slowly collected at the corner of her eyes; words couldn't seem to come out. That's when I yelled, "Forget it!" completely ignoring her emotions.

She then blurted out, "Your father was going to kill us!" I stopped everything I was doing and looked at her.

"Brianna, it was some things going on that you were just too young to understand."

"Like what" I asked. "You told me my father left me at birth."

She glanced up at me, "Brianna, please sit." I removed a box from the couch and sat next to her. She wiped her face and continued to explain, "It all started when your father, Geno was between jobs. Jewel was about ten and you were 6 months at the time. Anyway, one day when I got home from work your father was sitting on the couch drunk while you were sitting on the floor playing with your toys. The house reeked of urine so I picked you up and your diaper was soaked. When I asked your father why he hadn't changed you he became furious. I had never seen Geno liked that before. He slammed the beer bottle that was in his hand onto the table causing it to break. I was afraid of what he would do so I put you in the playpen. When I turned around that's when he smacked me to the floor. I was terrified. I tried grabbing the phone but he got it before I could reach it. He then pushed me into the wall, which left a knot on my forehead.

"As he continued to pound on my body like a punching bag, you sat there crying watching from your playpen. When Geno noticed that you were looking he stopped and immediately apologize to me."

I cut Debbie off before she could say another word, "Why didn't you just leave or call the police, I don't understand."

I listened as she tried to explain, "Until you go through physical abuse you'll never understand. This man had threatened my life. The scars he put on my body will never amount to the number of scars he put on my heart. I couldn't go to the police because they wouldn't do much but write up a report. A report wasn't going to stop Geno from hurting me. I just couldn't escape him. I was too afraid. Geno use to beat on me if he thought I was looking at another man or if another man was looking at me. He had some serious issues.

"One night he came home loud, drunk and smelling like women's perfume. When I told him to keep it down because you and your sister were asleep he got upset. Before I knew it, his hands were wrapped around my neck. I could hardly breathe until your sister came out of her room and hit him in the leg with her steal bat. Geno instantly let me go and grabbed his leg. As I gasped for air I could see Geno turned to Jewel and pushed her to the floor. Not knowing he was armed, I reached for the baseball bat that's when he grabbed his pistol from his side and started hitting me with it.

"The next day one of my eyes was shut and the other was black. When Geno left for work, he told me if I tried to leave he was going to kill me. I knew then that it was time for me to go, especially since he put his hands on my child. As soon as he left for work I packed as much as I could and left. I didn't want to go to my mother's because I knew Geno would go there first. Instead I drove to Fredericksburg, VA and got a motel. After three weeks in a motel money was getting low. I knew I couldn't go back to work because Geno would look for me there. I had no other choice but to put my pride to the side and take you girls to my parents' house. Your Grandma begged me to go to the authorities but I was too afraid to do so. I thought the police wouldn't do anything but convince me to take out a restraining order which wouldn't stop him from hurting me. My Dad gave me some money so I went back to the motel by myself. I knew if Geno found me there alone he couldn't hurt you or your sister.

"One evening when I returned to my motel room Geno approached me from behind. I tried shutting the door quickly but he followed, pushing me into the room. That's when he yelled, *Where are my kids*? I told him you two were away at camp. I tried to get up but he pushed me down and got on top of me and said, *Didn't I tell you I was going to kill you if you left me?* He then started choking me. The guest from the next room could hear Geno yelling so they called the police. Good thing two police officers were in the lobby at the time. They broke open the door and drew their guns on Geno. That night he was charged with attempted murder and several other charges. He's still serving time in prison today."

I closed my mouth and swallowed my spit, completely loss for words. I couldn't believe all of the pain my father had put my mother through. Now I understood why she didn't want to talk about the past. I felt bad for the horrible things I said to her but I still hated her for not being there for us. We just sat there for a couple moments in silence then Debbie leaned over to hug me. I moved back so that she wouldn't touch me. Debbie then looked at me and said, "You're so smart Brianna but stubborn, just like your father."

"Is that why you didn't come for us, because I reminded you of my father?" I asked frankly.

She shook her head then said, "Brianna you have every right to be upset with me for not telling you the truth but you can't hold that against me forever." I cut my eyes at Debbie then got up and continued to pack.

Jasmine Minter

CHAPTER SIX

The following week I agreed to meet Debbie for lunch. I still had questions that needed answers. When I arrived at the restaurant Debbie was sitting in the corner booth reading the local newspaper. "Hi Brianna," She said greeting me with a smile. I greeted her with a wave before sitting down. Debbie was so excited. She couldn't stop thanking me for coming. She took a sip from her cup and said, "I'm pretty sure you have questions about what we talked about last week."

I looked over at her and just stared for a few seconds. "Let me ask you this, when Geno was arrested why didn't you come back for us?"

Her head fell to the ground as I waited for her to explain, "Brianna at the time I was depressed and really strung out on drugs. I wasn't fit to take care of you or Jewel. I didn't know how to cope with the trauma so I turned to alcohol and drugs. It was no way I could give you and your sister the love that you all needed. I didn't

69

even love myself which is probably why I stayed in an abusive relationship with your father. For a long time I was insecure about my appearance because of my mother. She made me feel ugly because my figure wasn't what she called acceptable to society. I admit I wasn't skinny or fat but I guess the way I saw myself didn't matter to her.

"She used to say things like, '*Don't eat those chips get an apple instead. You don't want to gain anymore weight*' During dinner she used to give me smaller portions as if I was on a diet.

My mother always made me feel like I was too fat and I needed to lose weight to be accepted so I went on a diet. When I met your father things were great until he started complaining about my appearance. He would say, *You could use a little meat on your bones.* Then when I got pregnant with Jewel he called me fat so I was in a lose-lose situation. I didn't have the courage to leave your father because I didn't think I deserved better. The self-hate that I had developed for myself had me believing that I didn't deserve anyone. Anyway, I was dealing with a lot of issues at the time so your Grandma and I decided that it was best for you two to stay with her and Grandpa. When I found out that your Grandma was sick I stopped doing drugs. It was hard but I knew since I couldn't be the mother that I wanted to be at least I could be a good grandmother to my grandchildren one day."

Call me heartless but I still wasn't interested in anything Debbie had to say. I wanted to know more about Geno so I asked her what prison he was held at. She gave me a funny look before asking, "Why?" When I told her I wanted to see him face to face she thought it wasn't a good idea. In the middle of our conversation my phone starts to ring. When I answered, it was Ethan's after school care. The instructor informed me that Ethan hadn't been picked up from after school care and it wasn't the first time Jewel was super late. I made up some lie about Jewel having car trouble and that I was on the way.

That wasn't like Jewel, forgetting to pick Ethan up from daycare; something must be going on with her. As soon as I got off the phone with the instructor I called Jewel but there was no answer. I knew she wasn't working because she told me the night before she was taking off. I started to gather my things and that's when Debbie asked if everything was okay. When I explained to her that Jewel forgot to get Ethan from after school care she yelled, "Go get my baby." As I stood up to leave she grabbed my hand and said, "Brianna I 'm sorry for not telling you the truth. I was only trying to protect you!" I replied with a head nod then proceeded out the door.

When I arrived at Ethan's after school care he was sitting out front next to his instructor. I jumped out of my car leaving the engine on. "I am so sorry" I said as I grabbed Ethan's hand. That's when the instructor asked me if everything was ok. I told her yes but I knew she didn't believe me from the weird facial expression she gave me. I put Ethan into the backseat buckled him up and drove off. On the way to Jewel's house I tried calling her again but still no answer. I knew something was going on with her because Ethan's clothes were a mess. It looked as if he had gotten himself dressed.

When I arrived at Jewel's apartment, Dee was on his way out the door. Jewel'd been acting very peculiar since Grandma

Beatrice passed away. Of course Dee's negative behavior didn't help. All he did was get high. I was starting to believe that his bad habits were rubbing off on Jewel. As we entered her apartment I noticed garbage running over from the trash can, dishes piled in the sink and clothes all over the couch. I yelled her name from the front room a few moments later Jewel entered the living room. "Hey Ethan" She said as she bent down to kiss him on the cheek. From her appearance it looked as if she just woken up. Her hair was all over her head and she was half naked with just a t-shirt on.

"Hi mommy" Ethan's innocent voice spoke.

"Hey honey, what are you doing home so early?" she asked.

Furious, I yelled, "Jewel! It's 7:15 in the evening. Ethan gets out of after school care at 6'Oclock. Where were you?"

Her mouth dropped to the floor, "Oh my God, I forgot to pick him up!"

"Yes, you did!" I yelled. "And the instructor told me that wasn't the first time.

What's wrong with you Jewel?"

She tried giving me a poor excuse, "What? I may have been a few minutes late but I never forgot Ethan at after school care."

I rolled my eyes, "Whatever! Just make sure you're on time tomorrow." I leaned down to give Ethan a hug then left her apartment.

As I searched my purse for my car keys another car pulled up right beside me then a familiar voice said, "Excuse me Ms."

When I turned around I noticed Chase. I shook my head and said, "Okay, now I know you're stalking me."

He laughed, "I wouldn't say that, just a coincidence that's all."

I rolled my eyes and continued searching for my keys. By this time Chase had gotten out of his car and walked to the other side of my mines. "Where are my keys!" I shouted aloud.

When I glanced up I noticed Chase pointing into my car and there they were, sitting in the passenger seat. I didn't feel like waiting for a tow truck I just wanted to go home. "It's always something." I mumbled while walking over to the stairs.

Chase followed behind, "Don't stress it, my boy has his own tow truck company. He can unlock your door." Before he could say another word I told him no thanks and continued browsing through my phone trying to find a pop & lock. Before I knew it I heard Chase telling someone on the phone I locked my keys in my car.

When the call ended he turned to me and said, "They're on the way."

"Did I not tell you I didn't need your help?" I said to him with an evil look on my face.

He laughed as he walked closer to me then said, "Don't be so independent that you can't accept help when you need it."

I rolled my eyes and sat back down on the steps. Chase then sat a few steps down from me. "Don't you have somewhere to be?" I asked.

He leaned his head back then glanced up at me and responded, "No, I don't. Chase then moved a step closer to me.

"Dude, you just don't give up do you?"

He shook his head, "No." I laughed. Surprised, he looked at me and said, "Wow, I didn't know you could do that."

Curious I asked, "Do what?"

"Smile" He replied. I hadn't laughed since my grandma passed away. To be honest I had nothing to smile about. After a few moments of awkwardness Chase asked about Grandma Beatrice. When I told him she had passed away the day I left the park his entire mood changed. He showed nothing but compassion and remorse for me. I quickly changed the subject to keep from crying.

After about twenty minutes of chatting a tow truck had finally arrived. Chase approached the guy, greeting him with a hand shake. The guy then reached for his equipment from his truck and began working on opening my door. When the door finally opened I shouted, "Yes!"

Chase smiled and thanked the guy. As I got into the car Chase stood at the driver's window. He smiled and said, "Can I call you sometimes?"

I chuckled, "Oh is that why you helped me, to get my number?"

He answers sarcastically, "Of course." My mouth opened wide, I was completely surprised by his response. Chase's face dropped to the ground, "I'm just joking with you, but seriously I would like to hang out with you sometimes." I nodded my head and said okay as we both exchanged numbers.

Later that week I decided to visit Geno in prison, the man that ruined my family. I was a little nervous sitting there waiting to see my father whom I hadn't seen since I was six months old. I didn't have a clue what I was going to say to the man that nearly killed my mother. When he came out his face lit up with joy. I assumed he turned Muslim from his appearance but I could be wrong. I could see his nappy braids sticking out from under his kufi.

I didn't think he would recognize my face since my mother never sent him any pictures. It was like looking in a mirror. This man looked exactly like me or should I say I look like him. It was no denying me even if he tried. He sat across from me and just stared for a moment then he fixed his mouth up to say, "Hi Brianna." I sat there staring at him with anger in my eyes and hurt in my heart. It was an awkward silence between the both of us for about a minute. "Wow you're so…"

Before he could get another word out I stopped him, "How could you beat the mother of your kids?"

A little embarrassed, he glanced around, hoping no one heard me, "Brianna, please" He mumbled.

"No, answer me!" I yelled louder.

He attempted to grab my hand but I jerked back placing them into my lap. His eyes grew larger, "Brianna that was years ago. I'm a changed man."

I laughed sarcastically, "Man, a man doesn't put his hands on a female. You're a coward!"

78

I rolled my eyes and looked away as he tried to explain, "Look I'm sorry about what happened between me and your mom back in the day. There's no excuse for what I did. I was going through a lot at the time and I took my frustration out on the one person who loved me more than I deserved to be loved. I tried writing and calling your mom but she refused to accept any of my letters or phone calls."

He cleared his throat as he continued to explain, "I grew up in a household with a bitter mother who verbally and physically abused me. She felt that I was the cause of my father leaving us. I remember her coming into my room late at night just to beat me for something simple as forgetting to make my bed. Since I've been in prison I've been receiving counseling for the physical abuse I went through as a child. I never meant to hurt your mom Brianna, she was my best friend. At the time I was between jobs and I know that's not an excuse but that didn't stop me from putting my hands on her. Sometimes it takes a painful situation to make a person change and I guess that's what happened with me. I know this probably won't make any sense to you but prison saved my life. It gave me the counseling I needed to help me overcome my past. You'll be surprised how much damage your past could do to your future. The choices you make while you're young can influence your future tremendously."

My ears didn't want to believe anything Geno had to say but I listened anyway. When I asked him if he had apologized to my mom he said he wrote her so many letters begging for her for forgiveness but she never wrote back. He continued by telling me that Debbie wrote him once, blaming him for what happened to me my senior year in high school. I didn't want to talk about that painful moment so I got up and left.

CHAPTER SEVEN

The following day while browsing the web I came across a screenwriting contest. This was a huge opportunity that I couldn't pass up. It was no way I was going to end up another statistic, repeating the cycle of my dysfunctional family. I grabbed my notebook from the night stand and immediately started jotting down ideas. Two hours into writing I received a text message from Chase inviting me to the park to watch him play ball. He'd been texting and calling since I ran into him the other day. I needed the break so I decided to meet up with him.

After playing three games of basketball, Chase made his way over to me. He approached me carrying a book bag and water bottle while wiping his face with a towel. His body was drenched in sweat. Once he reached me he smiled and said, "I'm glad you made it Brianna. I thought I wasn't gonna see you again."

I laughed, "You keep playing like that and you won't."

He chuckled, "I see you got jokes, you just caught me on a bad day that's all." I smiled sarcastically, thinking to myself *yeah right*. Chase then threw the towel over his shoulder and joined me on the bench then asked, "How you holding up?"

"I'm okay. I've been writing everyday which helps."

He smiled, "You're a writer?" That's when I mentioned my dreams of becoming a filmmaker. After listening to my aspirations Chase became curious about the things I wrote about. I didn't feel comfortable discussing my personal business but that didn't stop him from asking the questions. "So are you going to tell me what you write about?" He asked. I wanted to be honest and say pain instead I simply replied with *things*.

He laughed "What kind of *things*?"

I turned to him with a smirk on my face, "Personal things."

He found humor in my response, "Well hopefully we can get to know each other a little better then maybe you could read me those things?"

"Maybe" I said. We sat there awkwardly waiting for one another to speak. Chase started to take off his sneakers then asked about my day. I told him it was good I guess but my answer wasn't good enough for him.

Chase took off his book bag and removed his flip flops then continued his lecture about how good life is, "You're alive, healthy and beautiful! What could be better than that?" He put a smile on my face then added, "You should smile more often, it looks perfect on you."

Blushing at his response I replied, "Okay if you can stop with the compliments we can hang out again."

He looks over at me with confidence and said, "I don't compliment to get anything in return, only when it's due."

The next day, Chase agreed to meet me at the Jefferson Park, one of my favorite spots in Richmond to look over the city. When I arrived I could see him at the top of the hill sitting on the grass. Once I reached the top, I saw Chase pulling out what looks to be a magazine from his bag.

I giggled, "What are you doing?"

He stood to his feet then reached for my hand, "You'll see, have a seat," he said. I sat down on the blanket and Chase did the same.

I was anxious and curious about what he had planned. "Seriously Chase, what are you doing?"

He smiled, "Well I understand that you love words so I thought that we could do something that you're passionate about while getting to know each other."

I was still confused, that's when Chase explained that we were going to cut out words to describe each other. "You're so corny," I said smiling as we both laughed.

While cutting Chase started asking question after the question. I felt like I didn't know much about him so I cut him off, "Enough about me," I said. "What do you want to do with your life?" He became silent so I spoke louder, "You do have goals, *right*?"

He quickly responded, "Of course I have goals. The shop is only temporary. Right now I'm in an internship program working to meet state licensure requirements to become an architect."

I gave a bright eye expression, "Wow, I'm impressed." We both giggled.

He cleared his throat, "What you thought, I played ball? Oh no let me guess, you thought I was a rapper?"

"I didn't say that" I replied. "But why an architect?"

Chase went on to explain that his grandfather use to flip houses back in the day. He also expressed his love for drawing buildings as a hobby which eventually turned into a passion. After two hours of talking and sharing the words we cut from the magazine it was time to head home. On the way to my car Chase asked, "So will I see you again?"

Jokingly I answered, "Maybe."

CHAPTER EIGHT

Several months had past and Chase and I had become really good friends. Jewel on the other hand wasn't doing so well. After Jewel lost her job she just wasn't the same person anymore. I got a call from my friend Markell, informing me that Jewel had a black eye. He told me that his boy overheard Jewel and Dee arguing the night before. When the phone hung up I called Chase and asked if he would meet me at Jewel's house and he said yes.

When I pulled up, Chase was out front waiting. He greeted me with a hug. We both walked up the flight of stairs towards Jewel's Apartment. I knocked twice before turning the door knob. When we entered her place it was a complete mess. It looked as if she hadn't cleaned in months. Her floor was so disgusting. I could feel my shoes sticking to the ground. We found Jewel lying on the couch wrapped in a blanket watching television. As we moved towards her she glanced up then quickly pulled the blanket against her face, covering her eye.

"What's up Jewel?"

Careless she replied, "Hey," without making any eye contact.

I walked over to her and asked, "What is going on?" That's when she covered her entire face with the blanket as if she was sleepy. "What's going on with you Jewel?" I repeated. She rocked back and forth as I waited for a response.

She seemed very irritated. "Nothing, I'm trying to sleep. What do you want?" She replied.

"Jewel, why are you covering your face?"

Lying she answered, "Because I'm tired."

I glanced around the messy apartment, "Where's Ethan?" Jewel mumbled from under the blanket, "He's in the back watching TV."

Curious I asked, "And Dee?"

Annoyed she replied sternly, "He's not here."

I got tired of beating around the bush so I got straight to the point, "What's this I'm hearing about you having a black eye?" She acted as if she had no clue of what I was talking about. "Jewel please, let's not play games. Who gave you a black eye?"

Jewel didn't say a word. Chase spoke, "Which way is the bathroom?" I directed him to the back.

I started to become impatient with Jewel so my voice grew louder as I called her name, "Jewel!" I attempted to pull the blanket from her face but she wouldn't let go.

"Stop", she yelled. Furious I asked, "Did Dee do this to you?" Jewel sat silently as I continued to question her, "Who did this to you Jewel?"

She sat up and pulled the blanket from her face and said, "Bri, it's nothing." I took a seat next to her. Chase had returned from the bathroom I was completely upset by then. The only thing that was running through my mind was *how could she let this man put his hands on her?*

I turned to her and said, "Jewel, how can you say it's nothing? You have a black eye! If a man hits you once he will do it again and the cycle will repeat until you think it's normal. Come on Jewel, why are you letting a loser like Dee take you through this? You have a child to think about!"

Sarcastically she replied, "Do I?"

My eyes grew wider. "Jewel let's not go there. You need to leave him alone. Look at you! Since Grandma died you fell off. You're always high off pills, you're forgetting to pick Ethan up from after school care and now you're letting a man beat on you. What the hell is wrong with you Jewel?"

Completely ignoring me, she rolls her eyes and says, "Whatever," then headed to the kitchen.

I continued to lecture her as I followed behind, "That's all you have to say is whatever?

Jewel, what about Ethan? If he's beating on you now, what's going to stop him from putting his hands on Ethan?"

While in the kitchen I noticed an empty pill bottle on the counter, "What's this?" Jewel tried to grab the bottle but I snatched it before she could. "What are you doing with pain pills? Did Dee give these to you?"

She gave me lots of attitude, "No," she says while snatching the bottle from my hand.

"Then why do you have them?" I asked. Jewel's nose flared up as she demanded me to get out of her face. Sarcastically I asked, "So you want to die huh?"

Jewel got upset at my comment and said, "What the hell you talking about Bri?"

"I mean you taking pain pills when you don't need them so clearly you don't care anything about your life. These pills can lead to other addictions."

Jewel chuckled, "What I look like, a crack head?"

I nodded my head, "You will, if you continue to take these.

I've read stories about people dying from pain pills drug overdose. Why would you want to harm your body?"

She dragged her feet and went back into the living room, "I don't even take that many." she replied.

At that point I was beyond pissed with Jewel so I let her have it. "Why are you taking them in the first place?" I yelled, furiously.

Chase spoke for the first time, "She's right, my boy's brother, died last year from popping pills. They're not good for you."

Jewel gives Chase an evil look, "Did I ask you?"

Chase got quiet and looked the other way. "Jewel, do you know what these pills could do to your nervous system and your kidneys?" Jewel sat there in silence staring at the floor. Nonstop I drilled her with facts, "Why would you want to harm your body? I just don't understand."

Careless, Jewel yells, "Whatever!"

"Whatever?" I replied. "That's all you have to say? Jewel, these pills can't cure anything you're going through. They just dull the pain for the moment and that's when you're going to find yourself taking more and more just to get a high. Before you know it, you're going to be taking something worse. What's going on with you? Is this your way of coping with Grandma's death? You know there's many forms of suicide and not all of them require dying."

She quickly responded, "Brianna, I'm not suicidal."

I shook my head and said, "So why are you taking prescription pills! Then you got the nerve to have this grown, no good for a man beat on you. Come on Jewel you're better than that. You saw what Debbie went through with Geno. Nothing ever gets better when you're in an abusive relationship. Get out before it's too late!

"Listen Jewel, all I'm saying is your life will become better when you remove negative people from it. I know you have a genuine heart and you try to see the good in everybody but not everyone is your friend. Good people bring out the best in you, not bring you down. Since you started talking to Dee you've become someone else. Not caring about your appearance or your child's.

Jewel that's not you! Dee not good for you! I'm telling you this because I love you and I know that you deserve better."

I guess Jewel didn't want to hear the truth. She jumped from the couch and got in my face and said, "You think you're better than me Brianna! You went to college and still have nothing! I guess you forgot I put my life on hold for you! If it wasn't for me your ass would be just another baby mommy with a bastard for a child." Chase glanced up at me confused while Jewel continued to run off at the mouth. "You're so quick to talk about my flaws but never talk about your own." She looked me up and down then directly in the eyes as she continued to bash me, "You're selfish, bitter and only care about your damn self Brianna." We stood there face to face, just inches apart. Then she yelled, "Just get out of my face."

Disappointed I replied calmly, "The choices you make not only affect you Jewel, but your family too! Remember that!" Talking to Jewel was like talking to a wall. I couldn't get my point across even if I tired. All she wanted to do was go back and forth with each other. I didn't have time to argue with her so I left.

Chase followed behind yelling, "Brianna wait up!"

I stopped at the bottom of the stairs before turning to Chase, "What?" I yelled. "What?"

He replied. "So now you got an attitude with me?"

I took a deep breath and glanced up, "Sorry, I just have a lot on my mind."

He started down the stairs, "Hold on." He reached for my arm as I tried to walk away, "Hold on Bri. Look, I'm sorry you have to go through this with your sister. I agree she needs help but don't stress yourself out. What good is that?"

I nodded my head, "You're right."

He pulled me in for a hug. "I've seen your sister before."

I glanced up at him as he held me in his arms. "Really" I asked. "Where?"

"I can't recall, but I never forget a face.

CHAPTER NINE

The following day Chase agreed to meet me at Pony Pasture near the river. When Chase arrived I was busy working on the script for the competition. He greeted me with a hug. I really didn't know how to tell Chase about the secret I'd been holding in for years. I sat there in silence for a second to gather my thoughts. Chase then broke the silence and said, "So what's up with you?"

I stared at the ground and took a deep breath, trying to get a hold of my emotions before I said anything. "I know you probably have some questions about the conversation I had with my sister yesterday," I said with a guilty conscience.

Chase removed his hat from his head, resting it on his lap and replied, "Yea I do."

"Well here's the truth. During my senior year in high school I was raped. I didn't tell anyone what happened because I was too afraid. Then one day my sister walked in on me vomiting, so I told her what happened. To make matters worse when she took me to the doctor we found out I was three months pregnant."

Chase rose up and moved closer to me. You could see the remorse in his eyes, "Damn, I'm sorry to hear that Bri. Who was the guy?" He asked.

"He was a close friend of the family who my Grandmother and Grandfather trusted.

When my Grandmother found out I was pregnant we talked about adoption and even me getting an abortion. Although Grandma Beatrice didn't agree with me having an abortion she felt that rape was an acceptable reason to have the procedure done. My Grandfather on the other hand disagreed. He wanted no parts of me killing a child. That's when my Grandmother confessed to making my mother get an abortion when she was fifteen and that really affected their relationship. I thought long and hard about giving Ethan up for adoption but my heart wouldn't allow me to do so. Jewel didn't want me throwing away a full scholarship so she gave her dreams up of becoming an actress and took temporary guardianship of Ethan while I went away to school. We both agreed that we would tell Ethan the truth once he was old enough to understand. The plan was to start my own film production company after college and my sister would star in my first film to help build her image as an actress.

I know it's a lot and I am sorry I didn't tell you sooner."

Chase spoke up, "No need to apologize. You did what you had to do. You've been through a lot and I understand why you didn't tell me. It has to be hard to talk about."

Relieved, I replied, "Yea, thanks for understanding."

Chase then looked me in my eyes and said, "You're not the only one with a past Brianna, you don't have to feel ashamed. We all have a past. Who am I to judge you for yours?" He took a deep breath, rubbed his forehead then looked away before continuing, "Growing up wasn't easy for me either. I lost my mother in a fatal car accident when I was just three years old. My father was a workaholic. He put his career before me. Of course I had the latest gear and newest games but I would have traded all of those things just to spend time with him.

"I know you're always telling me to express how I feel and to be honest Bri, that's hard for me being that my father never showed me how. The only thing he did for me was provide and we both know it takes more than that to raise a child. He never showed me what it felt like to be loved. Don't get me wrong I thank God every day for blessing me with a hard working father. I just wish he spent more time with me.

"For years it was hard for me to trust anyone until now. Till this day my dad lies about the simplest things so I distance myself to keep from being disappointed. Sad to say, but it is what it is. I respect you for keeping Ethan. Just make sure you don't hold on to that secret for too long. He needs to know that you're his mother and your reasons for doing what you did. I'm not perfect and I'm no saint but God saved me from a lot of things. Not having my father around much made things harder for me, mostly in the classroom. My grades really weren't the issue it was more so my behavior that teachers couldn't tolerate. To change things one of my teachers recommends putting me in a special education class to help decrease my negative behavior. She said to my father and I quote, *I believe a large setting maybe a distraction to your son and that's why he's acting out. I recommend that your son is placed in a smaller setting with fewer students to help decrease his negative behavior.* She even had the nerve to tell my father that I would receive monthly social security benefits if placed in a special education class."

"When the teacher mentioned social security benefits my father went off. He explained to her that he works hard every day and doesn't appreciate being bribed into placing his son into a special education class to receive government assistance. I'm assuming she thought my father wasn't financially stable because of my behavior or maybe because of my race. My behavior had nothing to do with the size of the classroom because I was completing my work with no problem.

My negative behavior was away to get my father's attention. I knew if I got in trouble he would have to come get me from school and spend the rest of the day with me. Crazy I know, but sometimes when kids need love they act out in a negative way to get that attention. I guess my teachers didn't have the patience to understand what was going on with me. If it wasn't for my grandfather or mentors I would probably be dead or in jail. The only thing my father taught me was how to provide.

"Anyway, I'm glad we got the chance to talk. It's good to have people you can vent to. You can't leave stuff covered up Brianna. Anything that stays covered never heals. If you leave a bandage on a cut too long it won't heal completely until you take it off. I'm not trying to tell you what to do but it seems to me that you're trying too hard not to be like your mother instead of being yourself. You're lucky to still have your mom around. Cherish her, you only get one."

After Chase told me that I felt bad. I was always complaining about Debbie and what she didn't do for me when I should've been cherishing her presence. It's so many people in this world that would do anything to have their mom or dad back and there I was complaining and taking for granted mine. My eyes started to water but my pride wouldn't let the tears fall. Chase started to noticed the pain in my eyes, "Brianna why are you so tough, don't you know it's okay to cry?" He says while rubbing my back.

"You're right Chase, it's just hard. I've never had a family so I just want the best for Ethan.

Society today is a scary place for a young black man. There are so many black men dying at an early age. Just the other day the news reported a little black boy being killed by the police and you know what Ethan asked me? He said, *Auntie, why did the police shoot that little boy? I thought the police supposed to protect us not hurt us?* Now Chase tell me what I'm supposed to say to a child when they ask me a question like that? I don't want my son to be killed for being mistaken as a criminal because he's wearing a hoodie or shot dead because his music is too loud.

We live in a society where cops get away with murder but a victim of domestic violence goes to jail for shooting warning shots at her abuser. Now what sense does that make?

I just want my son to live longer than me, that's all."

Chase spoke up, "Brianna, not all cops are bad cops and not all criminals are black.

Police officers *are* supposed to protect and serve. Criminals are supposed to commit crime and thugs are supposed to act as thugs. We can't complain about the system if we're not a part of the system. It's important that we vote and not just talk about making a difference but actively work and live towards making a difference." He paused for a second then said, "Brianna you can't categorize people by the mistakes of their peers or race."

I glanced over at him and said, "Tell that to society."

CHAPTER TEN

A couple weeks had past and things were going great. Jewel and I were taking turns keeping Ethan so that I could spend more time with him. Then one night Jewel came to pick up Ethan and she was high as a kite. I mean she looked horrible. Her shirt was falling from her shoulder, her speech was slurred and her eyes were fighting to stay open. I was so pissed at her. She stumbled into the house tripping over a step, "Hey Bri, where's Ethan?" she asked.

I stood there for a second and just stared at her, disappointed. *How could she be so irresponsible?* I thought to myself. I guess she got tired of waiting for a response so she rolled her eyes and moved into the family room.

She spoke in a soft tone, "Let's go Ethan." This was a sign that I needed to get my son back soon. If Jewel thought for one minute she was going to take Ethan while she was high then she has another thing coming.

I walked over to Ethan, grabbed him then turned to Jewel, "Go where?" I asked. Ethan puts his arms around me. I could tell that he was afraid.

Her voice grew louder as her words continued to drag, "He's going home!" she yelled.

Jewel reached for Ethan's arm but he wouldn't let me go. She yelled at him again, "Ethan let's go."

Ethan looked up at me. "Jewel, how do you expect to drive and you can barely keep your eyes open?"

Jewel opened her eyes a little wider. "I drove here didn't I, now come on Ethan I don't have all day." I whispered to Ethan that everything was going to be ok then Jewel moved closer to us and yelled, "What did I say?" Ethan glanced up at me confused. Jewel stumbled onto the couch. Her head fell onto the arm rest. She sat there slumped in the chair. Immediately I sent Ethan to my bed room.

When Ethan left the room I let Jewel have it. "What the hell wrong with you?" I said standing over her. Jewel struggled to stay awake. "Look at you nodding off, what did you take?"

Annoyed and offensive, Jewel denied taking anything. I stared at her hard searching for the truth. "Jewel you have a problem!" Jewel started to get comfortable, propping her legs onto the couch, ignoring my presence. I tried calling her name one last time but she was out cold, snoring. At this point I was beyond pissed! She was sound asleep so I left her alone.

The next morning when I woke up, Jewel and Ethan were gone. I was so over Jewel and her ways. I had just a week before my screenplay was due so I thought why not work on it. When I went downstairs to get my laptop I couldn't find it. I searched the house from top to bottom but still no sign of it. Then I remembered my laptop being on the table in the family room next to the couch. I really didn't want to believe that my own sister would steal my laptop but she was the only person in the house besides Ethan and myself. I tried calling her several times but she didn't answer. I was so mad. I needed someone to talk to so I had Chase meet me at Floodwall Park by the river.

When Chase arrived I was standing there looking over the river. I had a lot on my mind and Chase could sense it, "What's up Bri, everything okay?"

I was so hurt by my sister. I just sat there with my face in my hand and shook my head and started to vent, "I'm just so tired of Jewel and her crap." Chase became concerned so he asked me what happened. "I'm just so tired of having to deal with her problems."

Chase moved in closer then wrapped his arms around me. Tears crammed my eyes. I tried my best to hold them in but I couldn't. Chase catched each tear that fell. "I'm sorry you have to deal with this" He said while wiping my eyes. "Have you tired getting her professional help?"

I took a deep breath before responding, "I've tried but when I talk to her about it she denies that she has a problem."

"Bri you have to stop stressing yourself over your family decisions. Your sister is grown. All you can do is give her advice.

110

It's up to her if she wants to take it. You have to start focusing on you and your son before your family runs you crazy."

My voice cracked a little, "You want me to give up on my sister?"

Chase clarified his comment, "Of course not but what sense does it make for you to stress over something you can't control. Brianna you're so beautiful inside and out, don't let anybody steal your pride. Just keep praying for your sister. Things will get better."

"I hope so" I replied.

"Brianna it will! You're so strong and driven!"

I looked at him and said, "Pain usually drives you to be something better."

Chase nodded his head. "Let me ask you a question, why do you like meeting at historical sites? I'm curious to know."

I laughed, "It helps me appreciate the sacrifice that my ancestors had to endure so that I could be here today. When I'm going through a difficult time I like to visit these sites to remind myself that life could be worse. I guess you could say it's where I get my drive from." Chase stared at me and smiled.

After meeting with Chase I went down to the local pawnshop where Grandma Beatrice use to take us when we were little. "Good Evening", the store owner greeted me as I entered the store.

"Hello" I waved back and got straight to the point, "Did you happen to get any laptops in recently?"

The lady glanced down at her notes, "As a matter of fact I did," she moved from behind the counter and goes towards the electronics, "I got this one this morning."

Surprisingly it was my laptop, "Can I take a look at it," I asked. She said yes and handed it to me. I browsed through the laptop, checking for my work; unexpectedly it was still there, *What a relief,"* I said to myself. "How much for this laptop?"

The lady glanced down at the notepad and said, "$300."

"$300!" I replied with a bright eye expression. "But it's my laptop!" I explained my situation to the store owner but she refused to give me the laptop without receiving any money. She grabbed the laptop from my hands and placed it back on the shelf.

I didn't have $300 to pay for something that was already mines. The only money I had was for the screenplay competition and any extra money for emergencies. I needed my laptop so I had no choice but to spend the money for the competition. I went back to the counter, "Here you go." I handed her my chances of winning the competition. I was so angry at my sister. I knew that she had serious issues because she had never done anything like that before. It was evident that her habit was getting worse. When I got back to my car I tried calling her several times but still no answer so I drove over to her house.

When I arrived at her apartment there were two ambulances, police cars and a crowd of people surrounding her building. I could feel my heart drop down into my stomach. I jumped out the car without evening parking into a space. Attempting to enter her building, an officer immediately stopped me in my steps, "I'm sorry ma'am but no one is allowed pass this line."

There was police tape surrounding the building. I glanced around and noticed Ethan in the back of a police car.

I quickly hurried over; "Ma'am," an officer stopped me before I could reach the door. Without hesitation I pointed to Ethan, "That's my son! What's going on?" The police opened the car door and Ethan ran into my arms. He hugged me tight and started to cry. "What's wrong baby?"

He wiped his eyes and asked if he was in trouble for calling 911. I told him no. Ethan went on telling me that Jewel wasn't moving and neither was Dee so he called 911 for help. I asked the police where was Jewel, he said that the ambulance rushed her to the hospital. When I asked about Dee he said that he wasn't so lucky. I asked if he could give me more details that's when the officer said, "Looks like an overdose." Although I didn't care much for Dee I wouldn't wish death on anyone. I knew that he and my sister had a problem but I never expected for something like this to happen.

On the drive to the hospital I received a call from Chase. He saw my sister's apartment building on the news so he was a little worried. I explained everything to him as briefly as I could. I guess he could hear the pain and anxiety in my voice because he tried everything to keep me calm. He agreed to meet me at MCV Hospital then we hung up. All kinds of awful thoughts went through my mind. I just lost my Grandma so I couldn't bear losing my sister too.

When I arrived at the hospital I noticed Debbie pacing back and forth in the waiting room. I yelled her name from across the room. When she saw me and Ethan she moved towards us, greeting Ethan with a hug. Immediately Ethan asked, "Where's my mom?" Debbie bent down on one knee and explained to him that the doctor was helping her get better. It was no way I could tell Ethan what was really going on with Jewel. A few minutes later Chase showed up. He glanced around until he noticed the three of us in the corner near the water fountain. He called my name then rushed over.

Soon after, the doctor entered the waiting room calling out Debbie's name. Debbie jumped up from her chair, "That's me." He approached us and asked if Jewel was her daughter. She answered yes. Before he continued I asked if Chase could take Ethan over to the snack machine. I didn't want Ethan hearing any bad news about

Jewel. The doctor then explained that Jewel's over dose was caused by pain pills. He mentioned that they were giving her lots of fluids, pain medication and sleeping medication as she went through detox treatment. The doctor informed us that she was a little out of it because of the medication. He informed us we were allowed to see her once the nurse got her settled into her room. Both my mom and myself smiled, relieved just a little.

The doctor walked away while I stood there in disbelief. I needed some time alone so I left the waiting room and went into the chapel to clear my head. While alone so many questions ran through my mind. I wanted to know why God would allow my sister and family to go through so much pain. I remember Grandma Beatrice would always say, "Go to Lord for understanding, wisdom and guidance." So that's what I did. At that point I wasn't concerned about Jewel stealing my laptop. I just wanted my sister to be okay and in good health so I did what I hadn't done in a while. I prayed. Grandma Beatrice warned me about this. She would say, "Talk to the Lord all the time and not just when you needed Him." But I guess that was something that I need to work on.

I sat in the chapel alone for nearly thirty minutes praying for a full recovery then I felt a tap on the shoulder. It was Debbie, "You okay Brianna?" she asked.

I wiped the tears that had escape from my eyes and replied, "I'm alright. I just don't understand Jewel. She wouldn't have done any of this if Grandma was alive. It doesn't make sense. Jewel had always been the rock of the family."

Debbie nodded her head, agreeing, "Your sister is very strong but you know sometimes strong people need help too. Jewel didn't take your Grandmother's death too well and that's what I think lead to her drug abuse. Dee played a huge part but we can't blame him for everything."

"Whatever" I replied. "Dee beat on Jewel like she was nothing and had her taking drugs."

"Jewel is a grown woman and knows right from wrong" Debbie replied. "Maybe Dee introduced Jewel to drugs but I blame myself for her choosing a guy like Dee. I exposed her to an abusive relationship when I allowed your father to beat on me in front of her

I admit, that was my fault!

CHAPTER ELEVEN

The next day I went to visit Jewel at the hospital. When I entered her room I found Debbie sleeping in a chair right next to her bed. Tears crammed my eyes when I saw Jewel lying there with an IV in her arm and tubes up her nose. It hurt me to my heart to see my sister suffer. I couldn't understand why God would allow something like that to happen to such a good person. I mean she was not perfect but she was always helping others. She was just a genuinely good person.

I moved in a little closer so I could whisper in her ear, "Jewel, if you can hear me, I just want to tell you that I love you and I'm here for you."

I guess I didn't whisper low enough because Debbie woke up, "Morning Bri."

I gave Jewel a kiss on the forehead then turned to Debbie, "Good Morning, how's she doing?"

She paused for a second then sat up in the chair, "Not so good, Bri." I was completely confused.

"What does not so good mean?" I asked.

Debbie took a deep breath and said, "She had back to back seizures last night." My mouth dropped I was completely speechless. I sat down to gather myself. Debbie then placed her hand on my shoulder. Tears raced down Debbie's face as she tried to explain. I was in total denial. "She's going to be okay. It just hurts me to my soul to see your sister go through so much pain."

"Why Jewel, why?" I repeated, staring at her. Debbie tried cheering me up, telling me that two detectives came by and mentioned that they were investigating a guy they believed sold Jewel the drugs she took. The detectives also explained that the recent over doses in the city all track back to the same dealer. I was irritated at that point and could care less about some drug dealer. I jumped up from my chair and began pacing back and forth, "I told her Dee was bad news."

Debbie grabbed my arm, "Brianna calm down!" she said in a calm tone. "It won't change Jewel's condition but maybe it can help save someone else life if this guy is off the streets."

I rolled my eyes, "Whatever, I just want my sister to get better." I sat back down and that's when Debbie grabbed me, holding me for the first time in a long time. A tear rolled down my right eye as we both sat there in silence.

She then released me and wiped her eyes, attempting to change the subject, "So I spoke with your friend Chase yesterday and he told me that you were getting ready for a writing competition or something." She smiled as she continued, "I see you two are getting mighty close."

I took a deep breath as I wiped my face, "I was but I don't have the money anymore and Chase is just a friend."

She looked at me funny, "Alright now, if you say so. Anyway, that's huge. I think you should go for it."

Discouraged I replied, "I can't! I had to pay to get my laptop back that Jewel had pawned."

Debbie gave me a surprising look, "She pawned your laptop?"

I nodded my head, "Yup, it doesn't matter anyway. I can't leave Jewel like this.

She's done so much for me. I owe her my life!"

I could feel Debbie staring at me. "It's going to be okay, Bri" she said while rubbing my back.

I got up from the chair and yelled, "I have to go." I needed to clear my head so I left the hospital. Exiting the ER I came across a homeless man with a sign that read *Need Money 4 Food, to feed wife and kids* I only had $20 to my name after paying for my laptop but I remembered Grandma Beatrice use to say, "It is better to give than to receive." I knew my chance of entering the competition was never going to happen so I gave the man the $20.

After driving around for nearly an hour I found myself at Chapel Island Park, chilling by the river. I knew I needed to take the time to pray but I really didn't know how. I knew I needed

God to help my sister so I just starting talking, "God I know I don't speak to you as much as I should and I'm sorry but I really need you right now. My sister doesn't deserve what she's going through. Jewel really is a good person. She's done so much for me, my child and our family.

Anyway, what I'm trying to say is please help my sister! I don't care about anything. I just want my sister to get better."

Later that evening, Ethan asked about Jewel. He wanted to know if she was going to be okay. I told him that she was very sick then he asked if he could stay with me until she got better. My heart smiled as I answered yes. After putting Ethan to bed I worked on my project. Although I didn't have the money I still wanted to finish. I stayed up half the night and ideas flowed consistently.

The next day as I headed out the house to meet Debbie I noticed a letter in the mailbox. When I reached for the letter I saw that it was from Professor Cutler. I opened the letter; it was a card with a check for $800 inside. I couldn't stop smiling. What did I do to deserve this? I guess praying really does work. I couldn't believe it. God truly does work in mysterious ways.

"Miss. Brianna, How are you? I am so sorry for the loss of your grandmother. I know how very special she was to you. I hope that you're chasing your dreams as a film maker. I've watched you work so hard these last past four years and I truly believe that you will be the successful person you hope to become. Just keep God first, write your goals down and take steps each day to reaching those goals. I know how hard it could be finding a job after college so here's some coffee money to help you a little. I hope you're doing wonderful.

God Bless,

Mrs. Cutler.

When I arrived at the coffee shop Debbie greeted me with a hug, "I wanted to meet you here to give you an update on your sister."

Hoping I asked, "Any good news?"

She took a deep breath then said, "Well I got a call from Jewel's doctor today and he advised me to start looking for a facility for rehab. Although she's doing much better she still needs help. I know that this is hard for you Bri but we're going to get through this. I'm aware that you have big dreams and I want you to follow the dreams. I'll take care of your sister."

I shook my head, "I don't know Jewel's been there for me since day one. I can't just leave her like this. She gave up her life for me. I owe her!"

Debbie reached for my hand, "Honey, you can pay your sister back by following your dreams, Jewel would want that. I think it's time that you get legal custody of Ethan and start living your life."

I exhaled slowly, "I don't think I was built for this mother stuff."

She smiled at me and said, "Honey, you were built to last."

While in the coffee shop the news caught my attention. "Wow" I blurted out while watching. "What", Debbie asked.

"The police just raided some car shop for drugs."

Happy, Debbie replied, "Good, hopefully it's the guy that sold Jewel those drugs."

"Ssssh! Hold on I'm trying to hear, oh my God."

"What is it Brianna?"

"That's the shop where Chase works. Excuse me waiter, do you mind turning the volume up a little."

"Sure," He said.

The news reporter stated that detectives arrested, Aaron Johnson, owner of AJ'S Auto & Repair also one of the largest drug distributors in the area. According to news reporters the FBI had been investigating this shop for the past two years. I was speechless and pissed at the same time. I felt betrayed by Chase. He had to know what was going on. I texted him immediately asking him to meet me at our favorite pizza spot in Shockhoe Bottom. I was too upset to talk on the phone.

"Oh my God," Debbie blurted out.

"What's wrong?" I asked.

She looked me in my eyes and said, "Brianna, Aaron Johnson is your brother."

I sat back in the chair, confused then replied, "My brother?"

Debbie's head then fell to the floor, "Yes, your brother. Your father had an affair with Aaron's mom back in the day."

I was in complete distress when she said that. "I have to go" I said as I got up from the table.

When I arrived at the restaurant my emotions were everywhere. *How could he lie to me?* was the only question running through my head. I sat at the last booth towards the back. Ten minutes later, Chase walked through the door with a very distributed look on his face. He leaned over to give me a kiss on the cheek but I moved away before his lips could connect with my face.

"What's up with you?" He asked.

"What's up with me, what's up with you?"

He took a seat across from me and looked around to notice everyone staring at us. "First of all why are you yelling and what you talking about Brianna?"

I stared him dead in the face with my nostrils turned up. "You know what I'm talking about Chase."

He was completely confused, "Look I had a long day. I just found out the police shut down the shop til further notice so I don't have time for games."

My left leg was shaking like crazy, displaying how angry I was. "What do you mean just found out?"

He took a deep breath before explaining, "Bri, I'm just getting back from my internship in D.C. Remember I mentioned this to you the other day. I didn't know anything about the shop getting shut down until twenty minutes ago. Why are you so upset about it anyway?"

My voice grew even louder, "Because the guy that the police has in custody could be the person who sold Jewel the drugs and to make matters worse I found out the bastard is my brother."

Chase looked surprise, "He's your what?" He asked.

"Look it's a long story. Please just tell me you had nothing to do with what was going on at the shop?"

He sat back, rubbing his chin hair and calmly said, "You can't be serious?" I looked him up and down and rolled my eyes, not saying a word. "Brianna, why would you ask me something like that? You know I'm almost finished with my internship, why would I sacrifice everything I work for to sell drugs? Come on Bri." He shook his head and continued, "You really think I'd lie to you?"

I looked away and glanced down at the floor, "People lie to me all the time. What makes you different?"

He shook his head and licked his lips. "Bri, first of all I'm not everybody so stop comparing me to everybody that ever hurt you. You're so hurt that you don't know how to accept love when it's given."

"Love!" I shouted. "Please!"

Chase grabs his keys from the table, "Look when you get done comparing me. Give me a call because I don't have time for this. Not everybody is out to hurt you Bri." Chase got up from the table, gave me a kiss on the forehead then walked out.

Jasmine Minter

CHAPTER TWELVE

The following week I decided to pay Geno a little visit in prison. As soon as he approached the table I asked him about AJ, "Why didn't you tell me I had a brother?"

He sat down, glanced over at me and paused for a second. "Brianna."

Completely ignoring him I yelled, "You thought I wouldn't find out?"

He folded his fingers together and looked at me sarcastically wearing a smirk on his face, "This is funny to you?" I asked.

He reached over the table and grabbed for my hand, "Of course not Bri. I didn't tell you the last time because you didn't give me the chance. You just stormed out. Look, I was gonna tell you about your brother. I just wanted to tell you the truth about me and your mom first."

"So you cheated on Debbie?"

133

He covered his mouth with his fist and looked away, "Yes, when I met AJ's mom me and your mom were having problems."

"Wow, so you're just a deadbeat who cheats and beat on females?"

"At the time, yes I admit that. But I'm a changed man now."

I was done hearing anything Geno had to say so I cut him off, "Look, I don't know if you heard but Jewel's in the hospital for taking drugs."

He then yelled, "What?" A guard at the prison tapped him on the shoulder and told him to lower his voice. He barely turned around to the guard, giving him a wicked look.

"According to the authorities, *your son* supplied Jewel and her boyfriend with those drugs. Her boyfriend didn't make it but Ethan called the police just in time, saving Jewel's life."

Geno shook his head back and forth, "No, no, no!" He repeated, covering his face with his hand. He looked at me then said,

"Listen Bri, I'm so sorry you had to find out under these circumstances."

I smiled sarcastically, "Sorry won't change anything." He put his head down and stared at the floor for a moment. I started saying anything I could think of to make him feel bad. "Because of your decisions in the past, my sister nearly lost her life."

His voice over powered mine, "I admit, some of the decisions I made in the past have affected my children's future, but Jewel and AJ are both grown. Sorry if I may seem too harsh but they made their bed now they gotta lay in it."

My eyes were so watery you would have thought I was cutting onions. I couldn't believe what Geno was saying. My voice started to crack as I tried to express my feelings. "Jewel took my child in just so that I could have a better life. She doesn't deserve to be lying in some hospital bed."

Geno reached for my hand slowly, "It's not your fault Brianna."

"I know, but I could have done something. I saw the signs and I didn't do anything. I knew she was taking drugs."

"Brianna, it's hard to help a person who has a drug problem. You can do everything in your power to help a person but it's really up to them to get the help that they need. Don't be too hard on yourself. The most you could do for a person who's on drugs or dealing with any kind of problem is pray for them because the situation is completely out of your hands. It's hurting me to know that my first born is up in some hospital and my son is in prison because of it. If I made better decisions in the past, you're right none of this would have happened. I can't tell you enough how sorry I am for not being there for you and your sister."

He wiped his eyes as he continued, "A father is supposed to be his daughter's first love and his son's first example. I should have been there for you guys. Unfortunately, I can't turn back the hands of time so I have to accept what I've done. As for you, you have a choice to be whatever you want. Don't allow this situation to distract you from your dreams. Your mom reached out to me recently and told me about your passion for writing. Well, use the experiences you've been through as an opportunity to strive to be better! You've accomplished something that no one in this family has ever done; you graduated from high school and college. Let me tell you something Bri, that's something to be proud of."

I glanced at him and said, "Thanks."

He shook his head and hushed me with his hand, "No need to thank me. I am just grateful that I have the opportunity to sit and talk with you after all the wrong I did in my life."

I crossed my legs and glanced down at the floor, "I've been through a lot these last past months. From losing my Grandma, my sister almost dying, finding out the truth about you and my mom to learning that I have a brother. It's been rough but I got through it. I've grown and I guess that's why God took me through these difficult situations.

"Brianna everything that you're going through is preparing you for everything that you asked for." Suddenly, Geno stopped talking and smiles at me.

"What?" I asked.

He smiled and replied, "I'm just so proud of the woman you've become. You're beautiful, strong and very intelligent." His compliment makes me smile. "Brianna, I think you should go visit AJ."

I was taken aback for a second, "Why?" I asked. Geno then said he thought it would be good for AJ and me to talk. I smacked my lips and took a deep breath, "Talk about what? If I see this man in person God knows what I would do."

Geno cut me off, "Brianna please! Don't hate him for what I did. I'm pretty sure if he knew Jewel was his sister he wouldn't have sold her those drugs."

"So that's supposed to make me feel better?"

He shook his head, "No, no I'm not saying that. AJ was wrong for selling drugs I don't agree with that at all. I just think you two should meet."

I rolled my eyes, "I can't see that happening. Anyway, I have to go."

CHAPTER THIRTEEN

It'd been almost two weeks since I spoke to Chase. I was starting to feel bad for accusing him. In addition I was busy working on getting legal custody of Ethan being that Jewel had temporary guardianship. Not to mention searching for a good facility for Jewel to complete her rehab and therapy. That had to be one of the toughest decisions I'd ever made besides having to leave Ethan and go away to college. It felt surreal, but sometimes you have to do the things that you don't want to do because it's the right thing to do. I thought a lot about what Geno said and decided to visit A.J in prison.

Before heading to the prison I was en route to drop Ethan off at school. On the way there he asked so many questions to the point I became frustrated. "Why do you ask so many questions?" I said, while looking through the review mirror at him.

Ethan's head then dropped to his lap. I was upset with myself for getting frustrated with him. We finally made it to Ethan's school so I parked the car, turned to him and said, "I'm sorry Ethan. It's okay to ask questions. If you don't know something, don't be afraid to ask. Only those who are afraid to ask questions are afraid to learn.

He then said, "Why do I always have to hold the door for you when we go out?"

I smiled and said, "You better be lucky you're not old enough or else you'll be pumping gas too.

Seriously, it's what a gentleman is supposed to do. Put it like this, always treat a lady as if she's your mother."

He said okay then continued to say, "Can I ask you another question auntie?"

I replied, "Of course."

That's when Ethan bravely asked, "Are you my mom?"

My heart nearly ran out of my chest. I was in complete shock. His question threw me for a loop, stuttering I asked, "Who told you that?"

He replied, "I heard Grandma Debbie say it."

I shook my head. It was no way I could lie to him or hold on to this secret any longer. "Yes, I am."

His eyes became watery. "Why didn't you tell me?" He asked.

I reached for his hand, "I didn't know how. I can explain things better when you get a little order. You're just too young to understand." Hearing myself tell Ethan the exact same words Debbie probably told me when I was younger made me feel like a failure. It made me feel like I was repeating Debbie's bad parenting cycle.

After dropping Ethan at school I made my way to the prison to visit AJ. I sat there staring at the glass waiting to meet my brother for the first time in twenty years. Once he finally appeared on the other side of the glass all I could see was a younger version of Geno. We both picked up the phones that hung from the wall, "Who are you?" He asked.

"I'm Brianna, Geno's daughter."

His face frowned, "Ok, so what you want from me? I haven't seen my father in years" He stated.

I hadn't been there five minutes and already I was disgusted with him, "Look," I said firmly. "I'm not here to discuss Geno so I could care less about how you feel about him. I came here to talk about my sister."

He gave me an awkward stare, "Who the hell is your sister?"

"Her name is Jewel."

AJ seemed puzzled, "Who the hell is Jewel?"

"Don't act like you know don't know her," I said.

"Lady I'm not acting, I've never heard of her."

I paused for a second. "It's funny that you've never heard someone that you supplied drugs to."

AJ looked around, "Listen I don't know what the hell you're talking about. I never supplied drugs to anybody so you can gone head with that."

I smiled sarcastically, "You can deny it all you want but let me tell you something, because of you my sister nearly died. Tell me, how does it feel knowing you almost killed your own sister?"

143

AJ replied angrily, "Look, I don't know what you're talking about and if this is true how was I supposed to know that this girl you talking about is my sister? I don't do background checks."

I was furious by his comment. "That's why you shouldn't be selling drugs." I yelled.

"You almost killed your own sister. Don't you know when you sell drugs it's no different than killing the person? It's the same thing, they're just dying slowly. You disgust me!"

AJ tried to explain, "Look I didn't choose the streets, the streets chose me."

I couldn't do nothing but shake my head, "Don't give me that excuse!" I replied. "We all have a choice and you chose the easy route. You don't have to be a product of your environment that's what you chose."

His voice grew louder, "Listen If you gone preach to me then you can leave. I got enough on my mind. I had to do what I had to do to survive. My dad wasn't around and my mom worked two jobs just to take care of me. I couldn't handle seeing her work like a slave so I

144

made a choice. I didn't get into the game to hurt people. I got in it to survive. Things were getting worse and bills were piling up. I did what I had to. I was desperate."

"AJ, what you need to understand is that, sometimes things get worse before they get better. There are plenty of jobs out here. It might not be what you want but anything is better than nothing. You should never make decisions out of desperation but since you did you have to live with the consequences. It's always somebody out there doing ten times as bad as you so you can keep your excuses for causing other people pain. I just have one last thing to ask you."

His left eye brow rose, "What's that?" He said.

"Did Chase have anything to do with what going on at the shop?"

He found humor in my question, "Chase, please. That dude not bout that life." I gave him a nod and said okay.

When I got back to the house Chase was sitting on the porch. I couldn't say that I wasn't happy to see him. When he saw me he greeted me with a disappointing look. I felt guilty for the way I treated him. I was too embarrassed to look at him because I didn't know what to say.

Chase stood to his feet as I approached him, "What's up Bri?"

"Chase what are you doing here?" I asked. "I thought you were mad at me?"

Chase nodded his head, "I was, but I know you don't know no better."

We both laughed. "Seriously Chase, what are you doing here?"

"I came to talk to you. What, you thought I was gonna be mad at you forever?"

"Yea I did! I mean look how I treated you and you still wanna be my friend."

Chase grabbed my hand and directed me to the steps as we both sat down, "Listen, I don't know what kind of friends you're use to dealing with but you're not going to get rid of me that easily. I admit I was upset but I also knew that you had a lot on your mind. You just let your emotions get the best of you that's all.

Anyway, I have some good news." Chase hesitated.

"What? Tell me!" I asked anxiously.

He smiled at me and said, "I got a job offer in New York."

"Get out of here! Congratulations! When do you start?"

"Next week." He replied smiling. My smile immediately turned to a frown. "What's up

Bri, I thought you would be happy for me."

"I am happy for you" I replied, miserably.

"Good because I want you to come with me." He smiled waiting for my response.

"What do you mean come with you?" I asked.

"Why not Bri, you'll be able to focus more on your work, plus a friend of mines knows a music director that's willing to help and mentor you."

"Chase you're not understanding me, I can't leave my sister!"

"Brianna you're sister will be fine."

Chase looked away, rubbing his head then suddenly his voice grew louder, "What about you! All you ever do is worry about your family and their problems. Your sister is grown Brianna."

My eyes grew wide as I yelled, "You're right that's *family!*"

"Man, listen, you have to start caring for Brianna, take a chance for a change. You can't learn from your mistakes if you don't make any. You have a gift to write." Chase placed his finger on my heart, "That's your purpose Brianna. It's your weaknesses that helps people not your strength. The things that you've been through can help so many people. I believe that's why God gave you the talent to write."

"Why do you care so much about my future?" I asked. "Chase, you don't deserve a friend like me. What you need to do is go to New York and live out your dreams. I can't leave my sister; she gave up her dreams just so I could have one."

"And that's why you need to come," Chase yelled. "You owe your sister that much."

Chase then leaned over and gave me a kiss on the forehead. I stood there and watched Chase drive away not knowing when I would see him again.

Later that night Chase was shot and killed. Apparently, AJ took a plea to reduce his sentence. Instead of taking his sentence like a man he lied and spread a rumor about Chase being an informant for the feds. Although Chase had nothing to do with AJ's illegal business he still associated himself with those types of people which caused him his life. Losing Chase made me think twice about the people I wanted in my life. I've learned that you have to be careful with what type of people you surround yourself with because usually you pick up their traits.

Jasmine Minter

EPILOGUE

Two years later, I was sitting at one of the largest independent film festivals in Park City, Utah. Beside me sat Ethan to my right and Jewel to my left waiting patiently for the screening of my first independent film. After losing Chase I decided to take a leap of faith and pursue my dreams as a writer. I took all that I had which was the $800 Mrs. Cutler had given me and brought two one way tickets to L.A for Ethan and myself. The transition wasn't easy. We stayed at local motels and shelters because I couldn't afford a place of my own until I was offered a housekeeping position at one of the local motels. The manger there allowed me stay for a couple weeks until he wanted more than a work relationship so I quit.

After that I found myself working at a breakfast joint which only paid eight dollars an hour. It wasn't much but it was better than nothing. It was hard trying to take care of my son working for little to nothing but I needed the money so I did. I cried almost every night hoping things would change but it only seemed to get worse. Working at the restaurant wasn't too bad.

The best part was being able to put a smile on a customer's face. This one customer was always so happy. She came in every day at seven a.m. and ordered the same exact thing each day, egg whites, yogurt, a side of toast and a coffee with cinnamon.

I remember the day I got kicked out of the motel she gave me something that I needed the most, a smile. She always seemed so happy to see me as if she knew me. After two months of working I was fired. Apparently, my coworker reported me to my supervisor. She told him that I had been taking leftovers home for the past couple weeks so he let me go. All I could think about was if I made the right decision to leave Richmond. Times like that Grandma Beatrice would say, "When it rains it pours." Let's just say it felt like I was standing under a dam, drowning.

A few weeks went by and I was still jobless. Every day after dropping Ethan off at school I would go to the local park to write. Although my move didn't turn out the way I planned I still never stopped dreaming. I continued to perfect my craft as a writer by checking out books at the local library and studying film when I should have been looking for a job. Then one day while at the park I was approached by a lady. When I turned to look, I noticed it was the customer who always ordered coffee with cinnamon added. I greeted her with a smile as she joined me on the bench. "Hi, I haven't seen you in the restaurant in a while." She said.

My head slowly dropped to the ground as I spoke, "I know, I got fired."

The lady gave me a bright eye expression and said, "Oh no that's terrible! I'm sorry to hear that."

She went on stating she noticed my passion for writing from the notebook I carried. Turns out she was a college professor at USC school of Cinematic Arts. She asked if I was interested in writing film. I replied, "Of course." That's when she gave me her card and from that day forward she'd been helping perfect my craft as a writer and with my financial issues. This kind lady was also able to get me a job on campus as well as a small apartment for Ethan and myself. I allowed her to read the script I had been working on for months and she fell in love with the story. Soon after she invited me to her class where I began working on my first film. I never had anyone care about my well-being besides my grandmother and Mrs. Cutler. When I asked her, her reasons for helping me she said it was my character that reminded her so much of herself. She said, "I think you're impressive and have a bright future ahead of you!" To hear those words and know that someone is rooting for me gave me the courage to work harder.

Since things were going well for Ethan and myself, Jewel decided to move out to L.A. after rehab to be with us. Debbie on the other hand made the decision to stay in Richmond where she became an empowerment speaker for domestic violence victims. She shared her story with many in hopes of saving victims from abuse. I can honestly say that I am proud of her and the woman she's becoming. I think it's pretty amazing how God puts us in a place that we may not want to be but it's where we need to be. I could hear Grandma Beatrice voice as if she was still there saying, "It's your faith that will determine your future." And she was right.

It was also Chase who pushed me and wouldn't let me give up. He had inspired me to do something that I thought I could never do which was to live without fear and regrets. I think everyone needs at least one person in their life who believes in their dreams just as much as they do. Grandma Beatrice would always say, "Honey, God put people in your life for a reason, a season or a lifetime." Its funny how when you're a kid you pay no attention to the things your parents and mentors say until you're much older. My grandmother instilled in me so many wonderful things. I knew I had to make something of myself so I decided to break the cycle of my dysfunctional family by choosing to walk my own path and not the path of my generation. If I can do it, so can you!

ALSO BY JASMINE MINTER

Pursuing Justice: Only To Discover Pain, Truth and A New Beginning

www.ingramcontent.com/pod-product-compliance
Lightning Source LLC
Chambersburg PA
CBHW030334020726
47493CB00004B/1273